ASHLEY BEEGAN

Lucy's Coming for you...

How do you protect your child...from someone who doesn't exist?

First published by Ashley Beegan Author 2021

Copyright © 2021 by Ashley Beegan

All rights reserved. No part of this publication may be reproduced, stored or transmitted in any form or by any means, electronic, mechanical, photocopying, recording, scanning, or otherwise without written permission from the publisher. It is illegal to copy this book, post it to a website, or distribute it by any other means without permission.

This novel is entirely a work of fiction. The names, characters and incidents portrayed in it are the work of the author's imagination. Any resemblance to actual persons, living or dead, events or localities is entirely coincidental.

Ashley Beegan asserts the moral right to be identified as the author of this work.

First edition

Cover art by Jaded by Design
Editing by Aisling MacKay Editorial

This book was professionally typeset on Reedsy.
Find out more at reedsy.com

To Alex and Archie, for inspiring me everyday…I love you.

Contents

	Acknowledgement	iii
1	Summer	1
2	Summer	13
3	Summer	18
4	One. Two.	32
5	Summer	35
6	Summer	38
7	Lucy's Coming	45
8	Summer	47
9	Aaron	52
10	Summer	54
11	Summer	58
12	Summer	65
13	Summer	69
14	For You...	73
15	Summer	75
16	Summer	80
17	Aaron	83
18	Summer	85
19	Summer	93
20	Summer	96
21	Summer	101
22	Summer	106
23	Summer	111

24	Summer	116
25	Summer	122
26	Swanson	126
27	Summer	130
28	Swanson	137
29	Summer	141
30	Summer	147
31	Three. Four. I'm knocking...	150
32	Summer	152
33	Summer	156
34	Swanson	163
35	Summer	167
36	Summer	172
37	Summer	176
38	Summer	182
39	At Your Door...	187
40	Summer	189
41	Summer	194
42	Summer	200
43	Summer	207
44	Summer	216
45	Summer	220
46	Summer	223
47	Swanson	227
48	Summer	231
49	Summer	235
About the Author		243
Also by Ashley Beegan		245

Acknowledgement

There are so many people I need to thank who helped me bring this story to fruition over four long years! *Lucy's Coming for you* has lived only in my head for so long that I worried nobody else would ever get to know her, and it's the best feeling to see it finally in print as my debut book. However, without the help of those around me it never would have happened. To start with, my amazing son, Archie, for whom my love shines in this book through Summer's love for Joshua. My long suffering partner, Alex, who always keeps me motivated and inspires me when writers block hits. The awesome writing community who made sure I didn't give up when getting the story published just seemed impossible. My fabulously blunt beta readers who called me out on anything they saw. Aisling MacKay, my fantastic editor who made the story shine, I doubt it would make sense without her skills! And the world's best ARC readers who polished up my typo's. Last but certainly not least, Jaded by Design for putting together such an eye-catching cover for the perfect finishing touch! Thank you from the bottom of my heart to each and every one of you. You've helped a writer's dream come true.

1

Summer

For a moment, I thought about trying to escape. Her cold eyes stared straight into mine. They were like two emeralds. Bright, serene, and angry. We stood in a showdown position reminiscent of the wild west fights from old cowboy movies. Not that I would ever watch a cowboy movie.

The sound of the cheap clock infiltrated my muddled thoughts. It was to my right on the white-washed wall behind me, above my head. *Tick. Tock. Tick. Tock.* The clock was far too low in such a dangerous place. Didn't they ever learn? Unless absolutely necessary, nothing should be within reach here. Anything, without exception, could be used as a weapon.

Annoyance plagued my mind, briefly overshadowing the anxiety instigated by the owner of the green eyes. She was in her forties and still staring at me with intense focus. Despite this and the rising nausea which sat heavily within my stomach, I kept my head straight. My face was expressionless, not unusual for me, and my eyes were wide and unblinking. I needed to show confidence as my training informed me. I was on guard. I allowed a small smile to line my lips, disguising any evidence of unease.

As beautiful as the emerald eyes were, they were surrounded by a mass of angry, red welts. The wounds encroached upon her features, from her forehead to her chest. Each raised mark was surrounded by a patch of white, where there used to be smooth skin. They looked like small lava pools across her face. Both eye sockets drooped towards her cheeks. Her lips were nothing more than slits. It was as if someone had pulled the skin off her face in one fell swoop, like a child removing a Halloween mask. Except she had removed her human disguise, revealing the monster.

She was not my friend on this particular day. Some days, she would be my friend, and we would laugh and joke like two high school girls. She would show me her jewelry and her adult colouring books. She always wanted to brush my long brown hair, though I couldn't allow physical contact. I was ten years her junior and, in her mind, we were two *normal* young women. But not on this day. On this day, I was her enemy.

I knew it. I could feel it. She revealed her distaste for me through her unfriendly stare. Her anger. Her need to lash out and to hurt me. She didn't move but stayed as still as the painted human statues on the nearby cobbled streets of Derby city centre. My body stiffened as I attempted to move my legs forward towards the young woman with the cold eyes and angry red face. The narrow hospital corridor did not assist with the claustrophobia that grabbed at me from every angle.

The corridor opened out into the ward, but this was not your usual hospital ward. Everyone has been inside a normal hospital at some point, even if just visiting a loved one. No. This was the kind of hospital most people are lucky enough never to see. The red brick building wasn't impressive to look at from the outside but was modern and purpose-built to keep people inside at all costs. It lay on the banks of the River Derwent and was a short walk from my home city, the quaint east midlands city of Derby.

The key to the air-locked doors behind me was attached to my elastic belt. Many items were hanging from my belt, mostly keys and fobs for the maze of doors within the hospital, but there was also an alarm to be used in emergencies in case I was assaulted, or if I were to see someone else being assaulted. However, I could not go through these doors. If I'd made it to the other side, I would have been safe, but to turn my back would be dangerous. I shouldn't have been in that position, a lone patient between me and the ward, but rules weren't always followed, so there I was.

I knew I was being absurd. I spoke to patients like Lucy every day, but most were unlikely to attack me. It was as if an unknown horror was waiting for me if I proceeded further. My legs were laden with fear, as though all my blood had sunk to my feet, adding to their weight. I took small steps towards her. Beads of sweat made my palms sticky, whilst my lips felt dry. It was as if the natural moisture in my body had gravitated to the wrong places. I forced my lips to curve into a larger smile. It was my signature move when nervous, though not always helpful. I hoped it wouldn't irritate her further.

Whatever happened, I knew I must absolutely not let my fear show. That would have been dangerous. I needed to get past her with no issues. There was no going back through the locked doors, so I needed to take the other route to safety on the other side of the corridor. I needed to walk past her with as much confidence as I could muster. The weak did not last long in such a hospital.

"Hi, Lucy," I said, trying to keep my voice warm, and friendly, although I felt the opposite.

Lucy said nothing as I expected, remaining statue-like and cold. She continued to glare at me, making her anger clear. Her muted features made it impossible to read her emotions.

Her black hair was tied back, so tight and slick with grease it appeared to be stuck to her head. There were bald patches visible on her scalp, old scars where the skin had been badly burned. She still wore her nightie despite it being 2 PM, an oversized t-shirt stating *Mother knows best*. My mind wandered to her child. Lucy certainly did not know best as a mother, but I forced those thoughts out of my mind. My face needed to appear friendly, not disgusted, and never angry.

To get to the other patients who did wish to speak to me, I needed to walk past Lucy. I was their confidante, their voice, and their advocate. Like I used to be hers. I forced myself to walk quicker and with more confidence. I wanted to show her I was not a threat, but nor was I an easy target. She needed to know that I had taken her hint. I wouldn't talk to her again that day unless she changed her mind, which she often did.

Lucy's head did not turn as I got closer. Her unwashed stench stung my nostrils as I walked past her without getting too close. The nauseating scent of dirt, grease, and body odour hung about her in an invisible cloud. She continued to stare at the space I had occupied rather than allow her eyes to follow my movements. My heartbeat slowed as I walked by Lucy without being attacked. The nausea subsided, and I realised it relieved me that Lucy was not my friend that day. A pang of guilt overtook the anxiety. Not for the first time, I considered that I needed a new job. I was there to help after all, and I *wanted* to support most of my patients. I knew for the most part they were far more likely to be victims of crime than to be violent to me. However, I also knew what Lucy was capable of, and she would happily do the same to me if in the right mood. Lucy worried me, and for good reasons.

But as I made my way by her, Lucy's cold, lank fingers wrapped themselves tightly around my wrist. I jumped round so fast my vision blurred, and bile burnt the back of my throat as nausea threatened to overcome me. Lucy's grip tightened, her sharp, icy nails digging deep into my wrist. I should have known not to turn my back on her. I reached for the alarm strapped to my belt. Lucy was strong. Strong enough to be hurting my wrist, but she released me as soon as she saw the panic in my eyes. She smiled, revealing yellow teeth.

"Don't grab me, please, Lucy," I said sternly. She laughed a high-pitched, girly giggle and turned to the door behind her. She skipped into her bedroom, slamming the door shut. Despite attempting to show no fear, my hands tremoured. I swallowed the bile in my throat. The warm air of the hospital was pungent as it filled my lungs. The scents of medicine, sweat mixed with cheap deodorant, and food didn't help to ease my nausea.

I cleared my throat, trying to regain some sort of grip on my emotions. My hands were still shaking, and I needed a glass of water. I turned around again and continued up the white corridor. It felt shorter now that Lucy had gone. I supposed the corridor was brighter than the average hospital ward. There were hand-painted pictures of happy hillside and beach scenes with inspirational quotes stuck to the walls. They reminded me of the drawings I had on my own walls created by my son, Joshua. Though these images were not a child's artwork but the result of the patient's art therapy sessions. The room still felt clinical, though. There was nothing homey about Bluebell Ward, despite these feigned attempts. It certainly didn't live up to its bright and flowery name.

The corridor opened up to a communal living space with lime green walls. There were several couches and armchairs arranged in a U shape in front of a medium-sized TV. A dozen patients had spread themselves out on the furniture, all of them female. Multiple members of staff sat amongst them. Some were nurses, and some were support workers. Support workers cared for the patients in much the same way as the nurses, except they could not touch medication. Or at least they *shouldn't* touch medication. Two staff members sat on hard kitchen chairs across from the youngest patient, 17-year-old Aaliyah.

Aaliyah's every move was watched. Two members of staff were with her at all times, and one would even watch her as she slept. Aaliyah suffered from anorexia nervosa, depression, and severe self-harm tendencies. She was tiny and skeletal but lethal, at least to herself. She wouldn't hurt anyone else unless they were trying to restrain her from hurting herself. Self-imposed cuts and bruises covered her body. I saw a fresh, deep cut in the middle of her forehead near the hairline. It was about two inches long, angry, red, and looked in need of stitches. She clearly had not had a good day. I decided I wouldn't talk to her today for fear of distressing her further. She would approach me if she wanted to chat.

Before I had the chance to sit and say hello to anyone, another young patient approached me. Louise walked right up to me with zero concept of personal space. It was a problem

I found common among the patients and one I had always struggled with due to my need for wide personal space at all times.

Again, my hand sat near my alarm. I hadn't had to use it in my eight months of being an advocate, but I needed to be careful. I was constantly surrounded by instability, terror, and people who thought the unthinkable.

Louise's dark-skinned face was red and blotchy, more so than usual. She took loud, deep breaths, as if she were having a panic attack. Her skin wasn't burnt like Lucy's, but she had pink scars from deep cuts. Line after line of scar tissue from her forehead to her chin. There must have been fifty lines on each side of her beautiful face. At 21-years-old, her face was destroyed forever. She would never leave the house without people staring at her and instantly knowing she was severely damaged.

"Hi, Louise," I said, my voice soothing and warm. I was well aware of how important being calm was when talking to someone in distress, particularly if they suffered from disordered cognitive processes. Speaking in a calm tone was an attempt to convince a distressed patient into subconsciously following my placid body language. "Everything okay?"

"They're in there, look!" She pointed to the nurses' station next to us. The nurses' station was a long, soundproof room with an end-to-end window that overlooked the living area. Unlike its name suggested, it was not an area specifically for nurses since it was not where the medication was stored. Instead, it was a meeting area for all staff. Private discussions could be had, such as meeting arrangements, handovers, and quick updates if a particular patient became *poorly*, which is staff code for violent. Right now, though, the ward manager was sitting in there, smiling and talking with two women I'd never seen before.

"They're talking about me! They've been in there for ages. Can you ask them to come and speak to me, please? I can feel myself getting wound up, Summer. It's so rude of them to sit there talking about me, and all I can do is sit here and panic! You wouldn't like it, would you? They wouldn't like it!" Louise spat the words at me, her voice getting louder with each one. She was verging on hysteria. I struggled to take in what she was saying.

A nurse approached us, her steps brisk. "Louise, sit down! The manager and the ladies will come and speak to you when they are ready," she barked. From her tone, I could tell that Louise had already tried to talk to them numerous times. The nurse must have felt fully justified in speaking to Louise like that in front of me.

I'd seen this particular nurse a few times. Her name was Emma. She was blonde with always perfect hair. It was hard to tell how old she was because of the amount of makeup she wore. Some of which had dried into her skin, giving it a patchy look. I guessed she was around forty. She came roughly to the same height as me, so about 5'4. I'd noted on a few occasions that she appeared firm but fair. Though it was hard to tell. As an outsider with the power to report to authorities, most staff were on their best behaviour around me.

Louise threw me a desperate look, although she did as she was told and sat down. I noted a fresh cut on her cheek. I smiled at her, hoping she trusted me enough to leave it with me and stay calm.

I stepped closer to Emma and asked, "Who are they?"

Emma glanced at Louise and lowered her voice. "They're

from Louise's previous care provider. They're checking in and looking to arrange the next steps for her. They've been in there for about two hours. I'm not sure exactly what they're discussing, to be honest." She didn't sound like she cared too much about the subject or their conversation.

Although she was next to me, she didn't look at me once. Her eyes constantly moved as she surveyed the ward. Emma was distracted, her mind elsewhere. She was likely overworked and tired. She smelled like she hadn't made it home for a shower in between shifts. I took a step back as anger rippled inside me. Not directed at Emma, but Sue and the two women with her. Sometimes the staff seemed to forget they were working with actual people. Damaged people. People who were tormented enough as it was. Women who did not deserve to sit there and watch three clinicians discuss their lives with no involvement.

Yes, private conversations needed to be had. Patients cannot be present during discussions that may negatively affect their mental health. However, conversing for two hours behind a giant window right in front of Louise was not fair and not good care. It must have been extra torturous for Louise, with her severe anxiety building every minute. This was her freedom they were discussing. They could have had a conversation in an office downstairs where Louise was not forced to watch them. I knocked on the door of the nurses' station before using my key to gain entry, and smiled politely at the manager, Sue. She was another petite, milky-skinned blonde. However, Sue was pushing sixty with soft wrinkles lining her face and was much meeker than the defiant Emma. She reminded me more of a loving, smartly dressed grandmother than a stern ward manager.

"Hi, Sue." I smiled brightly, knowing she would not like me coming in here and undermining her. But she deserved it. If she had made a better decision on where to discuss Louise's care, I wouldn't have needed to undermine her. "I wondered if you could speak to Louise soon, please? She is getting very anxious as she can see you guys talking about her. Or maybe you could go into a private office so she can't see you, at least?"

My smile grew bigger again. I had no genuine power in this situation, other than the staff wanting to appear competent and willing in front of an outsider who knew how to report them, if necessary. An outsider who would be taken seriously if a complaint was made and who could make their lives difficult. Confrontation was never easy for me, though, and if Sue was to refuse my polite request, I wasn't sure what my next step would be.

To my immense relief, Sue smiled back. "Of course, yes! Poor thing. Tell her we will be with her in two minutes." She appeared genuinely concerned. I thanked her gratefully and returned to inform Louise. The tension in Louise's shoulders visibly eased. I smiled as she thanked me, feeling a bit more confident again after remembering why I was there. This was why I enjoyed my job...most of the time.

I spent some time chatting with a few of the other women about menial subjects, building rapport. Some patients started putting on their coats and shoes before standing near the exit door. They were being treated to a cinema trip to The Quad in the city. It was a creative center of Derby's historic cathedral quarter. It boasted a nice cafe and an art gallery as well as an indie cinema on the top floor.

I knew The Quad building well. Three years ago, fresh out of university, I presented life skills classes for adults with autism in one of their upstairs rooms. I analysed the patients who had been allowed such a treat. It was the quieter patients, the ones who were not as ill as the others still vegetating on the couch.

The patients often saw it as a punishment if they were not allowed to attend such outings. As if they were a child who wasn't being allowed on the school trip because of naughty behaviour. I got a lot of complaints about this type of event. It might not feel fair, but sometimes a patient was too much of a risk to the public and could not be allowed to leave the hospital grounds. Hence why they were in a secure hospital in the first place.

I noticed Lucy was not among the crowd. I wondered if that was why she was not my friend today. Maybe she blamed me for her missing out on the trip. The trust between us was well and truly shot. Thanks, psychosis.

I looked through the nurses' station window again. Sue and the other two women had left, and it had been around two hours since I'd spoken to Sue. It was time for me to move on to the next ward. Aaron Walker, one of two male nurses in the hospital, was in the nurses' station alone. I decided to go and speak to him about Lucy. I recognised him as a friend of a friend from my university days studying Psychology. I didn't know if he remembered me too, and I had never found an appropriate moment to discuss our university nightlife on the ward. I let myself back into the nurses' station.

"Hey, Aaron," I said to his back. Even though he wasn't yet looking at me, I smiled again and hoped he didn't now dislike me because I was an advocate. I wanted him to see me smiling to show I was still friendly. Plus, it was harder to say no to someone who was always nice and friendly. It was human instinct to be nice in return.

"Hey, Summer." He turned to look at me and grinned back, showing uneven white teeth through his dark stubble. He was tall, about 6'1, and his thick, black hair flopped over his forehead, partially obscuring his left eye. Aaron's paler than usual complexion made me wonder if he was sick. He still wore black guyliner around his eyes which had always accentuated his light skin, but there was a sweaty sheen to his cheeks. "Still going to Rednote?" he asked me.

"Oh god, no! Well, sometimes when I'm drunk enough!" I replied with a laugh. So he remembered me from our favourite student nightclub. "But I don't drink much these days with a child around. What about you?"

"Every weekend!" He winked. "How is the little one? Not so little?"

"He's six. So no, not so little! Makes me feel old!"

"You're not even thirty, shut up!" He pulled a mock confused face before retrieving his grin. "Anything I can do to help ya?"

"Yeah, actually, I wondered why Lucy Clarke hasn't gone to the show? She was acting a bit off with me earlier, and I wondered if it was me or if she's been ill again recently?" I knew he would understand what I was asking. *Has she been violent lately?* However, he looked confused for a moment. Then his dark eyes darted away as if he was looking around for an answer. I watched as his confusion turned to panic.

I wondered if Lucy had done something more serious and braced myself. If something serious had happened, I should have been told before entering the ward so I could protect myself from a particularly violent patient. However, his answer was not one I could have ever anticipated.

"Lucy Clarke? There is no Lucy Clarke on this ward."

2

Summer

I laughed at him at first. "I spoke to her like two hours ago."

Aaron looked uncomfortable, but I couldn't fathom why. It was a simple enough question. Surely he knew who I meant. There were 15 patients on the ward. As a nurse, he needed to know them all well enough to deliver medication.

"Lucy," I repeated. "Lucy Clark?"

He pursed his lips and looked deep in thought for a moment. Then, finally, he shook his head. "Nope," he said. "There's definitely no Lucy."

"Stop playing games, Aaron." I laughed again, convinced he was playing a trick on me.

"I'm serious, Summer. There's no Lucy." His face was sombre, and I began to doubt myself.

"You can't miss Lucy. She has burn scars covering her face," I said.

He looked deep in thought again. The word *overacting* sprang to mind.

"We don't have any patients with facial burns. There's Izzi, but only her hands are scarred noticeably. There are no scars on her face."

I crossed my arms over my chest and glared at him. A joke was fine, but I genuinely wanted to know how Lucy was doing.

"Her room is number 15," I said.

"Number 15 is empty," he replied without missing a beat.

"Show me then." I knew without a doubt that Lucy was in there. She hadn't left since our earlier interaction. I would have seen her on the ward.

"Come on, then," he replied.

I tried not to let my surprise show. I'd half expected him to decline. Yet, he walked straight out of the nurses' station and beckoned for me to follow. I willed my legs to move, but they refused. I had a bad feeling about what was going to happen next. Something was nagging at my brain, warning me not to go looking for trouble. I told myself I was being ridiculous. Of course, Lucy would be in the bedroom. I followed him, shaking off my doubts.

As we walked through the main lounge, Louise ran up to me again. "Summer!" she shouted in my face, making me jump back.

"Hi, Louise." I smiled at her, trying to recover from the scare she gave me. "Is everything okay?"

"Yes, they came to speak to me." She beamed now, all her earlier anxiety calmed. "They wanted to see how I was doing. Sue told them I was doing well!"

She reminded me of Joshua whenever he did well in school and came home with a good behaviour certificate. "That's great!" I told her.

"You are doing well, Lou," Aaron said. "I'm going to show Summer something. We'll catch up later." He continued through the lounge and I followed, despite my nagging reservations. *Stop being ridiculous,* I repeated to myself.

The lounge was practically empty by that point, with half the patients having left to visit The Quad. That left about half a dozen patients milling around the ward in various rooms. I wished I was going on the visit with the others. I got to accompany the patients on trips sometimes. It was my favourite part of the job, getting to see them happy and doing normal things. Activities that other people take for granted every day, such as shopping or going for a walk. I couldn't imagine having every aspect of my life be in the hands of others because I was ill. I would hate having someone else making my decisions for me because of something out of my control. It seemed so unfair, but then what else can the doctors do? The patients needed to be looked after somehow. They needed to be protected. And sometimes, the public needed to be protected from them.

I looked around for some sort of distraction as we walked silently to Lucy's room. Anything to stop the feeling of impending doom, which was getting stronger and stronger within my gut. The stench of some sort of burnt meat filled the lounge. The kitchen was right off the back of the room, partly open so the staff could watch patients as they used it. There was a sink, a microwave, and drawers full of paper cups and plastic knives. The cupboards were filled with food the patients had bought themselves. Sticky labels covered everything. To the back of the kitchen was another door leading to where the oven and proper cooking utensils could be found. If they had been behaving well, some patients were allowed to cook with supervision. Others were rarely allowed because of their history. Although, for those particularly ill patients, they didn't need an oven to cause harm to themselves. A patient once took me into a private room and simply lifted her sleeve. My eyes met with the most horrific sight. A single pen jammed right into a vein on her arm. That was three months ago, and I was still not over it.

But there was nothing to distract us, and we reached the corridor a few seconds later. When we reached her room, Aaron tried to open it. It was locked, and I knew right then he was right. The rooms couldn't be locked from inside, and staff wouldn't lock anyone inside their bedrooms. There was a safe room for patients who needed to be locked away. It was a padded cell with a shatter-proof window to the ward and an opening in the metal door to pass food through. It was straight out of a horror movie. People probably thought rooms like it no longer existed. Yet, it was still used as an alternative to overmedicating patients and, therefore, seen as the more humane option. Straitjackets were no longer a common item in the UK, at least, but the padded cell was still used.

Aaron jangled the keyring on his belt, looking for the key to Lucy's room. He had many more keys than I did. At least when he opened the door, we would see Lucy's things, and I would be proven right. Less than a minute later, he unlocked and threw open the door. The smell of bleach stung my nostrils. An unmade bed sat in the far right corner, and the chest of drawers next to it was open and empty. The closet by the opposite wall was also open, with just hangers inside. Clearly, this was not Lucy's room.

"I don't understand..." I fell quiet as words escaped me.

Aaron glanced at me. "You're probably thinking of a Lucy from another hospital?"

Cold fear grabbed hold of my stomach and twisted around

it, like Lucy's icy fingers around my wrist. I shivered at the thought of our interaction as one terrifying thought took over.

Is Aaron lying to me, or am I going insane?

3

Summer

I spent an hour visiting the male ward of Derby Hospital before I could finally leave for the day. I tried to put Lucy out of my mind, but the feeling of her stiff fingers snaking around my wrist was stamped into my brain. I looked down at my wrist. There were no marks.

It was real. It was real.

Fridays were usually a good day of the week for people. The last day of work for lots of office workers and contractors. The beginning of the weekend, time with family and friends. For me, Fridays were the worst day of the week. I never got to spend time with Joshua on Fridays because he was always at his dad's house. I was so happy he still got to spend time with his dad, but for me, Fridays sucked.

So did the Friday afternoon traffic. I weaved my blue BMW one series in and out of traffic along the dual carriageway, desperate to get home. I needed to be alone to sit, to think, and just *be* for a while. Ten minutes after leaving the hospital, I arrived at a car park in front of an immense building. The car park was enough for ten cars, five on either side. It was for flats one to eight, with two visitor spaces for guests. I noticed a FIAT Punto in the guest space. I would usually try to figure out which neighbour it belonged to, but not that day.

The front wheels hit the kerb with a thud, jolting me forward, but I barely noticed. For once, I didn't bother to check if the wheels were okay. I levered my short self out of the bucket seat and slammed the door behind me, clicking the key fob's *lock* button three or four times as I walked away. Cold evening air stung my face, and a damp smell hung in the air. It hadn't stopped raining for three days. That wasn't unusual October weather for Derby, which averaged at less than ten degrees celsius. It was my biggest gripe about living here. I hated being cold.

I leaped over the sludgy grass to reach the pathway leading to the colossal Jacobean building that soared in front of me. Gravel crunched under my thick-heeled boots as I rushed to the steps. Over a year had passed since I made this walk for the first time, with Joshua's tiny hand holding mine, his other holding Richard's. Our lives had fallen apart one month later. The flat Joshua and I lived in was small, but the 170-year-old building it was a part of was stunning. In a funny twist, famous architect Joseph Danbury originally built the building as an asylum. It stood within a ten-acre site and included the original chapel further down the road.

I hurried up the thirteen curved steps to the entrance. An unlucky number for some. I wasn't superstitious, but I had always been glad for the additional three steps that led to the great double doors. Engraved above those grand entrance doors were the words *ANNO DOMINI MDCCCLI*. The shallow part of me loved it, finding it poignant and elegant. I'd lived nowhere even remotely classy before. I grew up on a typical council estate with my mum and two brothers, one older and one younger. A hundred feet above the engraved words was the striking bell tower with a red brick column on either side. The building continued at a right angle past each column, albeit at a much lower height. Blue Staffordshire brick and stone detailed the red brick in a sectional pattern.

At the end of the gravel pathway, I fumbled with my key before finally fitting it into the external door of the old asylum. Once inside and out of the freezing wind, I took a moment to embrace the welcome warmth of the central heating system. My shoes tapped loudly off the antique flooring as I hurried towards the marble staircase that ran to the left of the vast entrance hall. The hall was stunning. The dark floor contrasted with duck egg blue walls. One solid dark oak door was on each side of the hall, leading to flats one, two, and three. The doors were not that old, but they were made to look antique. The hall always smelled earthy, although I'd never been sure why. An ormolu and cut crystal Victorian chandelier took centre stage of the pristine white ceiling. The icicle drops and rosette crown scowled down at me as I climbed each marble step, criticizing me. I was an imposter living amongst such opulence.

At the top of the staircase was a double door which conflicted with the grand hall. It was made from light oak and modern, and a sign of the rest of the building's decor. Externally, many original features had been saved, but the hall was one of few original interior features. Through the modern doors, the narrow corridor floor was covered with deep red carpet tiles and surrounded by plain, white walls. It reminded me of a budget hotel. I had been tempted to redecorate it myself and then feign surprise along with my wondering neighbours. Lack of money stopped me, and I wasn't sure if I actually had the balls.

I reached the third door along on the first floor, flat number six, and again fumbled with my keys for several seconds. My fingers felt much thicker than usual. They trembled, although I was unsure why. Probably anxiety. Maybe fear. I cursed before the key finally slid into the lock and turned. I walked straight through the door on my left to head into the living room. Relief hit me as my own belongings enveloped me like a comfort blanket. The beautiful antique blue paint on the walls, the pine table in the corner, the black leather sofa complete with cracked arms. None of it matched, but it was mine. It was home.

I threw my old handbag onto the floor, kicked off my boots and ripped off my socks, not caring where they landed. My bare toes squeezed into the soft, grey carpet underfoot. It had been a gift from my successful younger brother, Dylan, named after Bob Dylan. I grabbed my old laptop from the table and plugged it in to charge. It always needed charging. I left it and exchanged my black suit trousers for comfortable joggers and my white blouse for a soft, warm jumper. As it often did when I was preoccupied with work-related matters, my mind wandered to my eldest brother, Eddie. His actual name was River, but nobody could call him that. I was eleven years his junior, and I'm not sure when he changed it, but I'd always called him Eddie. I was also 11 years old the last time I saw him, so I was hardly a reliable source of information regarding his name. I'd tried to look for Eddie many times once I was old enough to do so, but I'd gotten nowhere. I even tried looking for his girlfriend, Marinda Tanda, but I didn't know where to look for her. I stopped looking once I found out I was pregnant. I didn't want him near my son. *Hypocrite*.

Guilt ate at me whenever I thought about Eddie. I was supposed to be an advocate for people like him, but that was work. I knew I was safe when I left the hospital at the end of any working day. I knew Joshua was safe. Work eased my guilt. If I helped enough people like Eddie, wasn't it the same as helping him? Better even, since I helped lots of people rather than one. Though Lucy had been playing on my mind since early afternoon, and I didn't leave the hospital until 5:30 PM. It was now 6 PM.

Maybe it was a good thing that I didn't have Joshua. I would be distracted by Lucy, anyway. At least I could be alone with my thoughts, but I yearned for a cuddle, as I always did. I didn't know what I would do when he got too big to cuddle me. I tried to convince myself I was glad for the peace, requiring it to untangle my mind from the web of Lucy-related thoughts. With a sigh, I flopped onto the couch and opened the ancient laptop. I only used it for job-related record keeping. My phone was much newer and worked far quicker for anything else. The laptop screen welcomed me with an image of bright, colourful flowers as it struggled to open the login screen. Whilst I tried to keep my patience with the slow machine, I sent Richard a quick text to ask if Joshua was okay.

As I waited, I considered what I knew about Lucy. She used to open up to me because she believed we were friends. Until a couple of weeks ago, when she had accused me of betrayal. She had screamed at me in the middle of the ward, to the point where staff had to restrain her. I had never had a patient be so angry with me. Usually, they got upset with others and asked me for my support. That was my role in, after all. I was to have no opinion of my own and provide factual information and support only. Lucy thought I had spoken to her nurses and instructed them to ignore her. It was untrue and unfounded, but unfortunately, psychosis knew no truth. It was not uncommon to lose rapport with a patient through no fault of your own or theirs.

My knee bounced up and down in frustration as I stared at the laptop, willing the login screen to appear. I needed my work files and reports. Every conversation I'd had with Lucy was recorded, despite what Aaron had told me. He was nearly believable, but I knew I saw panic and fear in his eyes. Thanks to working with pathological liars in several jobs after studying psychology for five years, I was a fantastic lie detector. I read facial expressions intently. I saw minute movements of the forehead that most others missed. I watched which way the eyes gazed as lies were told and in which direction oblivious hands pointed and waved. I noticed jittery legs, which bounced like my own did when I was nervous or anxious, an annoying habit I picked up from my dad before a car crash had taken his life.

Aaron knew who I was talking about. He knew Lucy. I could tell that much. But where she could be and why was he lying, that I could not fathom. I needed to ring my mentor, Natalie. She was my immediate supervisor, a thirty-five-year-old who lived in Birmingham. My supposed guide through being an advocate. The thought of calling her made me bristle with annoyance. I was forced to check in with her weekly, much to my dismay. Not only did I prefer to be left alone, but she had also made it acutely clear that I was her first supervisee. As a result, she was overzealous in monitoring me. I got it. She was trying to impress our big boss Alexia. I still disliked it.

I was more highly qualified and had far more experience

at working with people who suffered from mental health problems. She had no psychology degree and certainly no master's. She had been an advocate for barely a few weeks longer than me and, previous to becoming an advocate, only had around a year's worth of experience in mental health. On multiple occasions, she would tell me I was wrong about something where I knew I was right. She once told me to ignore it when I informed her a male patient was being mistreated. She said I was probably wrong, so monitor for now. I ignored her and reported the hospital to the CQC, the Care Quality Commission. Though I was still waiting on their response three months later.

Regardless of my feelings, she was officially my first port of call for any issues. But I couldn't call her yet. I would sound delirious. Plus, she would likely tell me to ignore it again. *Monitor for now.* I scoffed at the memory. I required some sort of concrete evidence first, so she had to listen and get Alexia involved. I'd only been an advocate for eight months, and I didn't want Alexia to think I was losing my mind either. So, evidence was a must. I would prefer to die than end up in a *secure* hospital as a patient. After witnessing the experiences of my patients and brother, I knew I was not as strong as them. I could never cope with the torture that their minds put them through on a never-ending basis. Too many of them never got better, trapped in nightmares decade after decade. There was no way I could ever do it.

I gave a long sigh of relief as the login screen finally appeared. Once logged in, I frantically clicked on a folder titled *DERBYC*, hoping the laptop would recognise my urgent need for information and suddenly decide to work quicker. I desperately needed a new one, but my employer, Rowan's

Advocacy, refused to supply them. And they were far too expensive for me to buy one on my wage. The folder eventually opened three times, thanks to my incessant clicking. I clicked on the separate files within the folder. I always entitled each with a date and nothing more.

Time dragged by as I waited impatiently for the files to open. After a minute or so, which felt like at least ten minutes, a multitude of excel documents opened all at once. I pressed *Ctrl* and *F* simultaneously on the largest file, a daily report named *Fri7:09* — Friday, the seventh of September. I visited Derby Hospital twice a week, on Mondays and Fridays. This report would have been created around three weeks ago. I entered the initials *LC* into the pop-up search bar. We were not allowed to write names in our reports for data protection purposes, meaning any notes on Lucy would be under her initials. When *LC* popped up on the report, a wave of relief washed over me. I was not crazy. I read the first entry to see what I had written.

Spoke to LC briefly today, but she is very ill at the moment. Mood was down, paranoid, anxious. She thinks I have betrayed her somehow - psychosis seems to be taking over. Did not want to communicate about her care and did not want assistance. Verging on abusive. Will try again next week if no longer confrontational.

So I hadn't woken up in a parallel universe. Lucy existed. She was not a figment of my imagination. I had spoken to her. I wouldn't have written it down otherwise. At least that's what I told myself. I clicked on the next excel file, which had since opened up. This one was named *Fri31:08*, one week before the other file. I searched for her initials again, looking for anything that might help me understand what had happened.

Friday, 31st August

Spoke to LC today. She was chatty and smiley. We are building good rapport-would like me to attend the ward round on Monday, which I've confirmed is fine if it is between 9 and 11 AM.

My heart skipped a beat. If I had attended a ward round meeting with Lucy, there must have been other people present. Other people who could confirm she was a patient and tell me where she was. I didn't recall Lucy speaking to other patients or even staff whilst I was there. This hadn't struck me as unusual, as I was on the ward for an hour or two twice a week. It would be easy for me to miss such interactions. So this meeting could be my only evidence to show Natalie. I opened another file to check.

Monday, 3rd September

Tried to speak to LC today. She did not want to talk or attend the ward round at all, with or without me.

Damn. We didn't go to the meeting together. My note seemed short and did not consider why Lucy missed the ward round. I assumed I couldn't get anything out of her during the visit. Plus, missing the meeting itself was not unusual. Ward rounds were formal meetings between the patient and their multi-disciplinary team, or *MDT,* to discuss how they're doing and the next steps of their care. Patients could request things such as new medication or section 17 leave from the hospital grounds. The regularity of ward rounds depended upon the hospital. It may be weekly, fortnightly, or monthly, which had always struck me as unfair. It was a chance for the patients to be involved in their care plan and what happened to them. Why should some patients only have the chance to request this from their RC once a month? I imagined four weeks was a hell of a long time to be detained in such a noisy and often violent environment, unable to even request leave.

Sometimes the patients liked to *threaten* the MDT with my presence at ward rounds. Some patients viewed them as the bad guys. They were in control of everything the patient did, from where they slept to whether they were allowed outside. Patients often thought that having me at their side ensured the MDT acted appropriately, for I was an outsider. I was not mentally ill. Therefore, I was to be respected. When the time came for ward rounds, a patient would often change their minds about me being there. If they had an enjoyable week, they might decide they no longer needed me to speak for them after all. Or if they had experienced a dreadful week, they may not want to go to the meeting. Any meetings Lucy attended would be in her patient file. This was the file completed by her MDT and kept in the nurses' station on Bluebell Ward. I needed to get my hands on that file.

Frustration hit me as I realised I was not back at the hospital until Monday. I didn't work on weekends, but I wasn't sure how I could wait. I was usually good about not bringing work home, but the whole situation with Lucy was so strange. Maybe I could visit the next day regardless and tell the staff I'd forgotten something. I could then go to the nurses' station to look for it. I was allowed access to a patient file if that particular patient provided their consent, and Lucy had never given me consent. But I didn't think she would care. Despite our fallout, I was trying to help her. Wherever she was, I had a bad feeling about it.

I looked at my watch. It was 7 PM, and far too late for me to visit the ward. I needed to put Lucy out of my mind. Otherwise, I would be no good to her. If I allowed myself to become too preoccupied, I knew I would not be able to sleep properly. And I did not function well on too little sleep.

I would happily sleep for ten hours a night if my schedule allowed for it. As it was, I probably managed six-ish hours a night on average and found myself exhausted most days. Often it was a struggle to concentrate.

I picked up my phone from the sofa and waved it in front of my face until it recognised my facial features. It took a second or two before the screen unlocked. I scrolled down the list of contacts and tapped the name *Kelly*. Kelly was a couple of years older than I but had been my best friend for over a decade now. A mutual friend had introduced us. The ringing went on for quite a while. I was ready to give up when she answered the call.

"Hello," Kelly answered in a gruff voice as if she were half asleep.

"Sorry, did I wake you?" I asked, although I was unsure why I bothered. She wouldn't care if I'd woken her. It was only 7 PM.

"Nah, just having a few drinks at home. What's up?" I heard her inhale deeply. She was smoking. My cigarette craving grabbed at my chest, and I took a puff of my electronic cigarette to shake it off. Clouds of sweet-smelling smoke filled the air around me.

"Nothing, I'm a bit bored." I wasn't sure how to broach the subject of what was wrong without sounding psychotic myself.

"Oh," she replied. "How was work?"

Fuck it, I thought. I needed to speak to someone about it before my brain exploded. And Kelly was my most trusted friend.

"Well, something kinda strange happened today."

"Go on." Kelly sounded a lot more interested. Most people were fascinated by my job, mainly because I didn't work in the average mental health ward. I worked with people who had been identified as *criminally insane* by the courts.

"So I was speaking to a patient, we'll call her patient Z, and then I went off to speak to some other patients. It must have been like, two hours later, bearing in mind this patient Z touched me and everything. Like she grabbed my wrist and hurt me!" I paused for dramatic effect. There was another deep inhale. "Anyway, two hours later, I went to speak to the nurse about her. He told me she doesn't exist! He said there's no Lu... I mean patient Zs, in the whole hospital."

"Dickhead," she stated simply. "He's obviously not good at his job if he doesn't know his own patients!"

I laughed loudly. I knew I could trust Kelly to make me think straight. Her blunt nature was always a help, and she saw life as far more black and white than I did. For me, the world was a mixture of colours. Yes, some things were black and white, others were shades of greys, blues, and whites, or even shocking pink. I needed to know why things happened, what made people do what they did, and I couldn't rest until I had the answer. Kelly didn't overthink any situation. I would be more like Kelly if I could control my intrinsic need for information. I would likely be a lot less exhausted and probably much happier. Maybe it was that simple. Maybe Aaron was simply wrong. Maybe he was not good at his job.

"But he showed me her room, Kelly. The room I thought was her bedroom, and it was empty." A chill ran down my spine at the memory.

"Maybe you're not good at *your* job!" She laughed, as did I. "Honestly, mate, it sounds like nothing. I wouldn't worry about it. He's an idiot, and you got your bedrooms mixed up. Or this patient Z lied to you, told you the wrong name or wrong bedroom or something."

"Maybe," I mused. I was unconvinced, but her straight-talking made me feel better.

After a few more minutes of general chitchat, I hung up. Whilst talking to her, a wave of calmness had passed through me, forcing away the anxiety that had been squeezing my insides all evening. Kelly was probably right, and if she wasn't, I'd find out on Monday. No big deal. I ate some leftover chicken pasta from the fridge, and then grabbed a hot shower to wash away the residual stress. The bathroom was my least favourite room in the flat. It was so cramped that we couldn't fit in a bath, which made Joshua sad. I'd promised him we would have a bath next time we moved house. That led to him constantly asking for a new house.

I let the hot water trickle over my body for some time, not wanting to get back out into the chilly flat. I didn't put the heating on too much when Joshua was away, not wanting to spend the money unless it was to keep him warm. Eventually, I left the warm shower and selected some fluffy blue pyjamas to sleep in. They were super warm, despite my hair still being soaking wet. I threw on some old soft slippers to match. I felt much calmer, but needed something extra. I sloped into the kitchen and grabbed a tumbler glass from the high cupboard above the oven. The kitchen was more stylish than I could have ever made it myself. The glitzy charcoal countertops with brilliant white cupboard doors were here when we moved in. I loved it. It wasn't big, but looked stunning.

I poured some Jameson's whiskey into the tumbler and then poured some more for good measure. I added some coke and brought it back into the master bedroom so I could sip it in bed, as I browsed Netflix for something easy to watch. My brain couldn't take much more deep thought. *Plus, the quicker I fall to sleep, the quicker I get Joshua back*, I told myself.

I ended up knocking back the large tumbler quicker than usual. My mind clouded over as I lay in bed, a silly comedy playing in the background. I got super hot as the alcohol filtered through my veins and stripped off my fluffy pyjamas, abandoning them on the floor next to my bed. A few minutes later, I was asleep. But not for long. She was coming for me.

4

One. Two.

I watched Summer stride around the ward as if she owned the place. She shimmied her hips as she walked like she thought she was God's gift. Her shiny brown hair reached her waist. She always wore it the same way. Long, straight, and unstyled. Sometimes it was all hocked up in a boring ponytail, even though her nose was too big for the style to be attractive. But mostly she left it down, as if she couldn't be bothered to do anything nice with it. Not like I would if I had such long hair. Mine wouldn't grow, but that was okay. I had my own new shiny hair by then. She didn't deserve her hair. Someone should chop it off. Maybe I'd chop it off.

The first time I saw her on the ward, she was shorter and fatter than I thought she would be. She had lost weight now, though, and was too skinny. She looked bony. Like she would be uncomfortable to touch. I bet she was single. Nobody would want to have sex with that. It would be like fucking a skeleton. And I hadn't even seen her wear makeup once since she started visiting the ward. She constantly smiled, attempting to appear genuine and nice. She wanted people to see her that way, but I knew the truth. No one else knew, but I could see it. The words were green when spoken, like a green mist escaping the truth teller's lips. The mist was purple when people lied.

Summer stopped smiling when she thought no one was looking at her. She was a destroyer of lives. She was fake and evil. It shone around her like an aura, deep red and so dark it was almost black. It was the aura of the devil. She didn't even *recognise* me. You'd think she would after all the time we spent together, but that's typical of her. All Summer thinks about is Summer. I was happy that she didn't recognise me. I'd hoped for it. I could take my time and mess with her head.

I'd told the ward all about her, so they knew not to trust her. I told the nurses and their assistants that she spreads lies and to tell her nothing. I told the patients that she tells the MDT everything they say.

Frustratingly, it didn't seem to bother her. *Typical.* She carried on coming. Every Monday. Every Friday. Like clockwork. I stayed well back when I could. I enjoyed staring at her, watching until the facade dropped. Her fear was obvious whenever a patient was agitated. Laughable that with her history, she feared the patients.

It wasn't obvious, at least not to people who did not have my gift. She always looked calm, but I knew the truth. I could smell fear. It had the metallic scent of blood, and she reeked of it. No one else could smell it. It was a gift of mine, one of many powers I'd possessed since my vision, like the power to see truth and deception. I couldn't wait until she saw what I had in store for her. She would be scared then. The dread in her would grow and grow until everybody could smell it. I was going to ruin her like she ruined me.

She would be so ugly she wouldn't want to go out in public ever again. I used to be ugly, but I changed that. I was clean, re-birthed, and free of my ugly skin. She would not have the same luck.

She spoke to an agitated Louise next. She looked concerned, as if she cared about Louise's stupid, insignificant problems. But I knew she didn't care. People like her didn't care about others. She was there for selfish reasons. Being near these pathetic souls, pretending to help them, pretending to care, it was all to make her feel better about herself. Deep down, she knew how disgusting she was. Summer could help her brother instead of these idiots, but chose not to. Which was all the evidence I needed to know that she was fake. A smile lingered on my lips as I wondered how she would feel if she were aware of how much I knew about her. If she knew I was there, watching her, always watching her.

5

Summer

Spidery wisps of moonlight reached through the blinds as I lay in bed. They danced and lingered on different objects, and my sleepy eyes followed them slowly across the room. The wisps spun around, a shadow in the doorway—a human shadow. Lucy.

She stared at me with her cold green eyes. She had pulled the hood of her black jumper tightly over her head, but I could still see those eyes lit by the moonlight. There was no life in them. The fire had disappeared. She was not friendly today. I could feel it, smell it, and taste it. Every fibre in my body told me to run.

I jolted up into a sitting position, desperate to create some space between us, and banged my head off the wall. *Shit, that hurt. I* wrapped the duvet tightly around my naked body as if for safety, but I didn't feel any more secure. Goosebumps covered my naked skin, and I cursed myself for taking off my pyjamas.

I watched Lucy for a moment and waited for her to say something. She was silent. I was unsure whether I should say something or wait for her to talk. All I could hear was my heart. *Thump. Thump. Thump.*

It was so loud I wondered if she could hear it. My breathing was ragged, and there was no pretending to be calm. It was my bedroom, not the hospital. She had invaded my space. The hair on the back of my neck had risen like tiny pinpricks, and my teeth felt cold against my tongue. I shivered hard. Why did the room feel as if it was below freezing? Yet sweat beads tickled my forehead as they slowly dropped into my eyes.

My dry lips moved as I attempted to say her name, but no sound came out. I tried to move again, but my body refused to obey. The room spun, and I blinked a few times, trying to clear my head. My face was sticky with sweat. I wanted to close my eyes and pretend it wasn't happening and that she was not here, but I couldn't look away.

A giggle escaped her deformed lips, the high-pitched laughter of a child, and I didn't feel bad for her anymore. I no longer wanted to find her. I wanted her gone. The laugh got louder. The air was so thick with evil and her greasy stench I struggled to breathe. I raised my hands, pressing them tightly over my ears as the laughter slammed my eardrums. Louder and louder until it penetrated my brain, and I couldn't take it anymore.

I squeezed my eyes shut and heard myself whisper, *no, no, no* repeatedly. A rustling sound broke through the noise, and I forced my eyes back open. Lucy was moving, and yet her legs did not move. Instead, she glided rapidly towards me. *What the fuck was going on?* Bile rose in my throat as she came within inches of my bed. I could not move. I sat and watched with my hands clasped over my ears, elbows pointed out as a hopeless defence. My bedroom was not a large room, and she was across the grey carpet and on the opposite side of my bed in seconds. She was still laughing as her grossly burnt hands reached for me. I closed my eyes and prepared myself for pain, a gurgled scream piercing the air between us. And the laughter finally stopped.

6

Summer

I raised my hand to rub the thumping ache at the back of my head and willed it to disappear. There was no lump, and Lucy was gone. One minute she was inches from my face. The next, I opened my eyes, and she had disappeared.

I *had* heard a thud, and I *had* banged my head. The pain shooting through my brain was proof. The soft bed sheets and duvet still protected my shivering, naked body, pulled up tight around my chest. I looked at the bedroom door where she'd first stood. It was closed as it always was when I went to bed. I couldn't sleep with the door open. So Lucy was never there. She couldn't have been. Yet the stench of her greasy, unwashed hair still hung heavy in the air.

I had to make sure she was gone. I flicked on the bedside lamp, the warm glow and familiar objects calming me. My second-hand TV sat on top of the pine drawers adjacent to the bed. The cute elephant teddy Joshua had bought me last Mother's Day sat next to me on my *Paris* bed sheets. The framed picture of Joshua and I watching dolphins in Lanzarote was on the bedside table. My anxiety eased as the familiarity of my surroundings soothed me. I snuck my hand down to the side of my bed to grab my pyjamas and hurried to put them on whilst still under the duvet.

"Hello?" I called out, feeling silly, and yet terrified that I might hear a response. Deathly silence greeted me. No laughing, or breathing, or footsteps. Thank God.

I needed to get a grip. I'd never had a nightmare so real. My ears still rang from the evil laughter that had penetrated my brain. But what if it wasn't a dream? My patients told me about their hallucinations all the time. I had one sixteen-year-old patient who saw a blood-covered witch whenever she felt stressed out. The witch told her to hurt herself, and the girl did so to make the witch go away because she was so terrifyingly real. Another patient spoke to God like he was sitting on the empty chair right next to him. And then there was my brother and his devil. These hallucinations were completely real to the person experiencing them. I'd never had a hallucination before, despite my fear of becoming ill like my brother, but I guessed it would feel like what had just happened.

I grabbed my phone from the bedside table. It was two o'clock in the morning. I couldn't call Kelly this late. She wouldn't be impressed if I called her in the middle of the night over a nightmare, for God's sake. *Fuck this.* I needed to get out of the flat. I needed to be around people. I gingerly got out of bed as if Lucy were still hiding somewhere. Every time I made a noise, I froze, and listened for a second. I removed my pyjamas and quickly threw on some clean underwear, a pair of old jeans, and a thick black jumper before grabbing my car keys. I didn't know where I was going, but I needed some fresh air.

I ran from my flat to the car park, still on edge from the

dream or vision or whatever it was. There was nobody around, yet I felt as though I was being watched. I shivered and cursed myself for forgetting my coat. It was freezing outside. Once safely in my car. I locked the doors and drove off at speed. I drove nowhere in particular initially, but eventually went to the twenty-four-hour supermarket. It was a ten-minute drive away, and I knew it would have bright lights and some other people. Not lots of people, but still better than being alone. Better than my flat with no Joshua. I needed to get the food shopping done whilst he was away, anyway. There's nothing worse than having a bored kid around whilst you're trying to shop or an over-excited one throwing everything they see into the trolley.

I parked right at the front of the store in the parent and baby spot. It wasn't something I would normally do without Joshua, but I was still pretty freaked out from my dream, and the car park was dark. Besides, few parents would be shopping with kids at 2 AM. With my conscience eased, I left my car and jogged over to the trolleys, keen to get inside and wander around in the familiar, safe environment. In my younger days, I probably would have gone to a bar. Now, at almost thirty, my priorities had shifted. The loud noise of a night out and the following three-day hangover did not appeal to me. However, that night was an exception. If I'd known anyone who would be up for a night out at 2 AM, I would have called them.

There were one or two other shoppers in the supermarket. As I entered the first aisle, I attempted to remember what food I needed for the week rather than think about what happened earlier. Or *the dream,* which I was pretty sure it was. *No, it definitely was.*

I eyeballed the ridiculous amount of different vegetables

that lined the aisle, trying to remember which ones I needed. I was in a world of my own and didn't hear any footsteps behind me or feel the presence of another body. Not until icy fingers gripped my shoulder. *Lucy*. My breath caught in my throat as I spun on my heel to face her again.

"No!" I squealed. I tried to sound stern but could not keep my voice steady.

"Whoa! It's me. I'm sorry. Are you okay?" Instead of Lucy's sharp eyes, I gazed into the dark eyes of Aaron Walker.

"Oh shit, sorry, Aaron. Shit. I was in a world of my own then!" I could not stop cursing as I tried to calm my heartbeat. A rush of heat spread across my face, and I looked at the floor. *Please swallow me up.*

"It's okay. Are you okay?" He looked concerned. My face flushed further, and I wished he would laugh at me or make a joke like he usually did.

"Yeah, I'm fine! Well, actually, I had a horrible dream, so I went shopping to take my mind off it." I giggled at how daft I sounded and flashed him a smile in some vain hope of convincing him I wasn't crazy, despite my actions earlier.

"Ah, that sucks! I've just finished work. I had to stay late." He rolled his eyes. The hospital was always understaffed, and people often had to take extra shifts or stay until a bank nurse arrived. "Why don't we go for a drink? I can take your mind off it more than shopping!"

I laughed at his offer. I couldn't remember the last time I had an impromptu drink offer in the middle of the night. It's not like the stereotype of single mothers getting drunk every weekend is true. I never had the time. Most of my child-free time was spent sitting around missing Joshua and looking at the chores I should do whilst he was gone.

I looked down at my old jeans, suddenly self-conscious in his presence. "I'm not dressed for a drink!"

"We can go to my mate's bar. No one in there will be dressed up. You'll fit right in." He winked at me.

I supposed it couldn't be that bad, and I could see what he had to say about Lucy after a few drinks.

"Okay, sure, why not!" I said with a grin, pushing down the nagging feeling in my stomach. I walked away from the few items I had managed to get in the trolley.

We talked about some memories of nights out as students as we drove back to my place to park my car. Neither of us mentioned the time we had kissed outside a nightclub as students. He came inside the flat with me to grab my coat. I still didn't want to be alone in there. The ten-minute walk back to town was quiet at first. It was just Aaron and I strolling through the frosty night air. But as we got closer, more and more people milled around. Most were falling around in a drunken stupor, getting kebabs and taxis home.

I'd forgotten how much Aaron could make me laugh. He was quirky at times. Some mutual university friends thought of him as strange, but I didn't mind strange. People thought I was strange, as an advocate for murderers, rapists and stalkers. His jeans were super tight and paired with a long Nirvana t-shirt. He wore black eyeliner and a large silver earring in his left ear, which stretched the piercing hole to the size of a penny piece. As we walked by the pubs we used to frequent, I remembered him dressing up as Captain Jack Sparrow once on a night out. It wasn't fancy dress anywhere. He then wore the same costume for about a month's worth of nights out, purely to make people laugh. Well, I'm pretty sure it was a conversation starter, and he was able to pull lots of women. His movements when he spoke were sometimes like Jack Sparrow, not as theatrical but somewhat similar.

It was around 3 AM by the time we reached his friend's bar. I looked up at the bright letters lit in neon orange above the door, spelling out *Charlie's*. I'd been there before with my own friends. It was a tiny place, usually frequented by lovers of indie rock and nowhere near clean. But the music and atmosphere were always great.

"Don't worry. He'll stay open until about 6 for me!" Aaron winked at me again.

I smiled at how he was showing off for me. I asked for a double vodka with soda water, a splash of lime, and a shot of tequila. He looked surprised.

"Have you forgotten how I can drink?" I laughed. "Well, until I got pregnant!"

I might not get the chance to go out drinking often, but I certainly made the most of it when I did. Plus, I hated being sober and surrounded by drunk people. We sat in the corner chatting about mutual friends and drinking. The front door of the bar was locked by then, but there were around ten other people still inside. Everyone was laughing and joking, having a good time. A couple swayed together on the tiny dance floor, holding each other up and giggling.

The drinks tasted metallic and flat, but I didn't care. I felt tipsy within an hour and couldn't remember the last time I'd laughed so much. Aaron made me feel so comfortable. I ordered more vodka and shots for us both. Our legs rubbed against each other as we sat drinking and laughing together. He caressed my thigh, and I didn't push him off. At 5 AM, I allowed him to walk me home. I didn't stop him from following me into the flat. I didn't stop his lips from reaching for mine, either. Or his icy hands from slipping up my top and closing firmly around my breasts. Instead, my nipples tightened, wanting his attention. I was on a high, drunk and happy with a funny man who was easy on the eyes. Fuck it. Real life could wait until tomorrow. I'd forgotten all about Lucy.

7

Lucy's Coming

Summer didn't see me as I watched her wander slowly around the shop. It was fun to catch her outside of the ward. I had to stay well back, as there weren't many people around to hide behind. Even still, I was pretty sure she wouldn't notice me. She appeared to be in a world of her own, and I looked different now, anyway. I'd taken off the mask to hide. I knew she wouldn't recognise me without it.

She looked tired. Her face was white, and black bags marked her eyes. She wore fading jeans with a scraggy old jumper. I wondered why she was here in the middle of the night rather than in bed. She stood in front of the vegetable aisle, but didn't appear to know what she wanted. As usual, she was indecisive. Weak. I wondered if she ever thought about me. I reckoned she'd forgotten all about me and the hours we'd spent talking. The times we'd shared.

A figure caught my eye, and I turned to see a man. I couldn't see his face, just his profile. He stood at the other end of the vegetable aisle, watching her too. So I watched him for a moment instead. He was a tall man with black hair, dark jeans that were much too tight, and a baggy black hoodie. I couldn't place him from this angle, but he looked familiar. He must have felt my stare because he turned and looked straight at me.

Shit! Aaron. What was he doing here?

He must not be allowed to mess up my plan. I rapidly changed my shocked expression and smiled at him instead. But then I remembered I wasn't wearing my mask so he wouldn't recognise me, anyway. Yet despite my missing disguise, his face turned pale against his dark stubble. He cracked open his mouth as if to say something. Did he recognise me? I risked it. I raised one hand and waved, enjoying how much I was freaking him out.

He turned back to look at her. Shit, was he going to tell her? No. He wouldn't be that stupid. Still, I turned and ran down the aisle where he could no longer see me. I slowed to a brisk walk and calmly strolled out of the supermarket. I didn't want the burly security guard to think I was a thief.

My body shook with adrenaline, but I laughed once outside. I probably sounded hysterical, but so what? The look on Aaron's face was priceless! I ran around the corner of the supermarket car park and down an alley to where my old Punto was parked. I had to get out of there, sharpish. I could always wait for Summer at her flat.

8

Summer

The morning light seeped through the blinds. It danced on my eyelids, and I groaned as I struggled to open them fully. The pain in my head did not help matters. I glanced over at Aaron. He lay in the bed next to me, snoring softly. I couldn't help but smile despite my head feeling like a tiny person was drilling into my brain. A small pang of guilt pulled at my stomach, but I pushed it away. I refused to bother with any regret. We'd had fun as two consenting adults, a lot of fun.

My throat felt like sandpaper. I reached out to grab the glass of water next to my bed and gulped it down. It soothed my dry mouth and made the drilling in my head a bit more bearable. The one thing I regretted was not asking Aaron about Lucy. I had enjoyed myself too much, and Lucy had gone completely out of my mind. Aaron being drunk had been the perfect opportunity. I needed to know if he'd somehow forgotten who she was or if she was safe on the ward. Safe for her, but safe for me, too.

Do I really need to know? Can't I forget what happened? Forget about Lucy?

I pushed the thoughts aside. I needed to know I wasn't crazy. If Lucy existed, then I wanted to help her and make sure she was okay. If she didn't, then I had to figure out what that meant for me. And, if I was hallucinating, what that meant for Joshua. That settled it. It was vital that I knew what had happened to Lucy to protect Joshua. I looked back over at Aaron and watched his chest move up and down rhythmically. I tried to figure out how to bring Lucy up again. He stirred and half flicked his eyes open before closing them again.

"Come here," he whispered. His muscular arm snaked around my stomach as he prised his eyes open again. "Good morning." He smiled sleepily. "I've been waiting years for this."

His smile widened into a grin as he reached up to kiss my cheek. I laughed and lay with him for a moment, enjoying the feeling of his powerful arms around me. I slid down, so my face rested against his warm chest. The small hairs tickled my cheek, but I ignored them. I couldn't ask about Lucy right now. It had been a long time since I cuddled an adult, and I didn't want to ruin the moment.

We lay there for half an hour, alternating between talking and just being. But that was about as long as I could manage before getting up and taking a hot shower. As nice as it was, I couldn't lie in bed for long. Even with an adult to cuddle, I got bored. It was a side effect of becoming a mother. I ignored his pleas to stay in bed but promised to buy him breakfast at a cafe down the road from my flat. *Barbara's Baps* was a greasy spoon that made the best cheese toasties I'd ever tasted. Perfect for a hangover.

The winter sun was warm on my face as we walked down the street. We dodged the puddles from the night-time rainfall and joked about the previous evening's antics. He reminded me about my terrible dancing as I tried not to blush. *Barbara's Baps* was one street away, so it didn't take us long to reach the cafe's blue and white front door.

Aaron gripped my hand and led me inside. I enjoyed the gesture, though it was not something I would normally allow to happen. It wasn't normal for me, but I liked the human contact. The one person I would usually allow to touch me was Joshua. I lived for his little arms to be wrapped around me, but I rarely hugged anyone else. Not even my own mother, for instance, and never would I hug either of my brothers. I saw Dylan at Christmas, and would likely never see Eddie again.

The cafe was a small building. It was previously a mid-terrace home and, as a result, did not have much space downstairs. There were six plastic tables dotted around in three uneven rows of two. Cheap waterproof checked cloths were draped over the tables, matching the blue and white colour scheme.

The counter was at the back of the room, and two women stood behind it, chatting. Both looked to be in their early fifties. They were rotund with greying hair, thick Derbyshire accents, and wore the same blue and white plastic aprons. They looked like sisters.

Four builders wearing yellow hard hats and matching high-vis jackets sat at the table to the left of the entrance. They joked and laughed loudly at each other's expense. Aaron led me to the right to take a seat on the bench furthest away from the door. I decided against a cheese toastie today and ordered a full English with an extra sausage and toast. Aaron ordered the same. I was supposed to be dieting to squeeze back into my skinny jeans, but I needed to soak up the alcohol. I had to pick up Joshua at lunchtime, and it was already eleven.

Our food arrived promptly and, halfway through our breakfasts, I still hadn't asked Aaron about Lucy. I needed to know before I picked up Joshua. I wanted to put it out of my mind. It was then or never.

"So," I smiled at him slyly, not sure how to word my question, "are you going to tell me the truth about Lucy yet? Because you're a terrible liar."

Worry lined his face for a split second before he forced his smile to return. But it was long enough for me to notice.

"There's nothing to tell. If we had a Lucy, I would know." He shoveled more sausage into his mouth.

"Aaron, I've checked my notes, and I record *every* conversation with *every* patient. I have had many conversations with *LC*," I said, attempting to sound jokey rather than confrontational. I smiled at him as I watched his face. Part of the reason I'd studied psychology may have been that I was naturally good at reading people, but I was not so good at confrontation.

"We do have some LCs. Izzy's proper name is Laura Coughlan." He dismissed my evidence with a mouth full of egg and bacon. "Why are you so bothered about one patient, anyway?"

"The dream I had last night that made me go shopping in the middle of the night? It was about Lucy." I looked away, not wanting to see his face when he got to thinking I was pathetic. Or even worse, that I'd lost my marbles.

"You….you saw her?" Aaron's voice was unsteady, and I looked back up at him. There was no smile now. His face had turned an even paler shade of white, the black stubble on his jaw was more pronounced than usual.

"Well, I dreamt I did. I think it was a dream, anyway. It was so real. She was in my room, and she sort of floated towards my bed…" I trailed off as I realised he was gawking at me with his mouth wide open. I had expected him to laugh and tell me I needed to chill out. Instead, he jumped to his feet, pulled some notes out of his pocket, and dropped them onto the table. I looked up at him, my face still and calm. I was used to keeping a straight face when shocked. It came with working in mental health.

"Sorry," he stammered, "I…er…I've just remembered that I have a shift at lunchtime. I have to go."

"I can give you a lift?" I offered, but he was already halfway out of the cafe. The noisy builders went quiet and looked at Aaron, and then at me sitting alone. I faced my head down towards the table so they couldn't see the red sheen I could feel appearing on my warm cheeks.

What the hell was that about? I had hoped for reassurance or an answer that would stop my mind constantly whirring about Lucy. But I'd ended up even more mystified. Something had happened to Lucy, and Aaron knew what. I needed to get my hands on that file.

9

Aaron

Aaron reached his flat at 11:45 AM, thoughts of Lucy racing through his brain. His breath heaved in and out of his chest. He wasn't used to running so quickly. *Fucking Lucy.*

It took a lot of effort to push open the heavy door to the building. He was glad they'd ended up at Summer's flat. It was much nicer than this dingy hell hole. He ran up two flights of grey stairs and finally slowed to a walk when he reached his corridor. His chest couldn't take any more running. The hallway had its usual aroma of damp and dirt. It made his stomach churn after eating most of that massive fry up. His flat opened straight into the living room with no entrance hall to speak of. He sat down on his battered couch, his head in his hands.

Stupid. Stupid. Stupid.

He tried to catch his breath before his lungs gave up altogether. He needed to calm down and try to think. Lucy must be following him. He was sure now. It wasn't a coincidence at the supermarket last night.

AARON

Lucy had also been at the cafe.

He had spotted her through the restaurant's window, watching them from across the road. She had been watching them, just as Summer was talking about her. It was as if Lucy had known Summer was asking questions about where she was. But why him, and what did she want? He kicked himself for going back to Summer's the previous night. What if Lucy had followed them there and he had put Summer in danger? No, wait, didn't Summer say Lucy had been in her bedroom before the supermarket, was Lucy following Summer? Confusion impaired his mind as he struggled to think straight.

He jumped up off the couch and raced to the window, which showed a view of the busy front street below. His flat was right off the centre of town, and he could see Derby Cathedral looming close by. He scanned the street, but Lucy wasn't anywhere to be seen. So where was she if she hadn't followed him home? A jolt of panic ran through him as he realised she may still be watching Summer. *Shit.* He had to warn Summer. But he couldn't tell her the truth. She would call the police. Maybe he didn't have to say it was Lucy. A crazy ex might do. She probably wouldn't believe him, but at least she would know to be more wary. He was especially concerned about Joshua after what Lucy had done to her own child.

He took his phone out of his pocket, having to stretch his leg to do so because of the tightness of his jeans, and searched for Summer's number. He thanked God he'd saved it last night as he typed out the text.

10

Summer

I struggled to concentrate as I waited for another driver to allow me to turn right into Richard's street. It might have been the alcohol from last night or Aaron's response to my questions about Lucy's whereabouts. I had no idea why he would have reacted in that way, and I didn't have time to think about it. I needed to concentrate on Joshua, but the questions refused to leave my mind.

A friendly driver finally allowed me to turn, and I pulled right up on the kerb outside Richard's semi-detached house. I took over most of the pavement, trying to ensure other cars could get by on the tight side street, then I grabbed my phone to call Richard. We got on better than when we first split, but I still refused to enter his house. He answered his phone as though he was surprised at my call.

"Hey, I'm outside," I said in my usual neutral tone.

"Oh, okay." Again with the surprised tone despite pickup being the same time every weekend. I bristled with irritation, but shook it off. One thing I'd learnt was to pick my battles with Richard. He was a good dad, after all. Though he kept me waiting for another five minutes before the door finally opened. Joshua ran outside, and my heart soared. All was well with the world again. He could barely move in his padded red coat and skinny jeans. I hated skinny jeans on young kids. They were so uncomfortable. I'd rather he was in comfortable joggers, but Richard preferred he looked stylish. I rolled down my car window as he ran up to it.

"Hi, baby!" Simply looking at him made me much happier. "How are you? You okay?"

He nodded and planted a wet kiss on my forehead before pulling open the rear door to jump into his booster seat. Richard followed him out. He wore his slippers and his dressing gown as a coat, which made him look much bigger than his actual slight frame. He was tall but skinny with it. His thick black hair was abundant with gel.

"Tell Mummy what you ate," Richard encouraged Joshua.

"I ate pasta!" Joshua shouted in triumph.

"Wow! Well done!" I exclaimed, my enthusiasm a tad over the top. "With what sauce?"

"Urgh! No sauce!" He stuck his tongue out and looked at me like I was mad for suggesting pasta should be eaten with sauce. "I had cheese with it." He gave me a big grin. He was so proud, but I fought the urge to roll my eyes.

"Oh, right. Okay, well done, baby." I flashed him another smile.

Richard attempted to help him with his seatbelt, but Joshua batted him away impatiently, insisting he could do it himself because he was six. Six going on sixteen. He said goodbye and gave Joshua a tight hug before closing the rear door.

"Bye, Daddy." We waved to Richard as we drove away.

Joshua chattered about his day for the whole twenty-minute

drive home and repeatedly told me he loved me. The immense comfort I felt at being with him again was unbelievable. I hated being away from him. I hated sharing every weekend and only getting two full days with him a month, thanks to work. I hated not having every one of his birthdays with him and sharing Christmas. I hated seeing our ex-babysitter in his second home, pregnant with his younger sister. It should have been me with a swelling stomach, not her.

When we reached home I allowed Joshua to choose a film to watch. We settled down for a cuddle and to watch Lego Batman for the 127th time. I decided to enjoy the rest of my day with him. I could think about Aaron and Lucy later. Joshua and I didn't get much time together, so I always made the most of it. As soon as we got comfortable, I noticed a new text message notification on my phone from Aaron.

Aaron: *Sorry, I had to run off. I completely forgot I had a shift! Can we meet later? Need to tell you something. And no, I'm not married! Don't panic :)*

I threw the phone away from me and tried to concentrate on the film, even though I could likely have recited most of the scenes from memory. But I considered my options as Joshua lay next to me, his sweet head on my lap. He giggled every so often at the film and looked up at me to make sure I laughed too. I tried to figure out if I wanted to see Aaron. I wanted to know what he had to say, but felt as if I was digging into an open wound. How deep could I go before it became infected?

I hugged Joshua tighter. Maybe I could stay in this little bubble of Joshua and me. I didn't need to get involved further. I could believe Aaron and move on. That wouldn't give me closure, though.

We ate plain pizza after the film, followed by bath, book, and bed. He squished himself into me as we lay in his bed together.

"Don't go, Mummy," he said as he did every night. "Stay with me."

I stayed with him and wrapped my arms around him tightly. I didn't ever want to let go. The familiar scent of strawberry shampoo and natural sweetness calmed me completely. If I could have chosen a moment to get lost in forever, it would have been that one.

"Mummy, I have an important question." His serious blue eyes looked up at me.

"Go on then," I said.

"How many miles away is Africa? Because Daddy said that's where lions live, and I don't want to be eaten by a lion." He looked up at me solemnly as I tried not to laugh.

"It's thousands of miles away," I kissed his forehead. "Now go to sleep."

He settled back into my arms. Within minutes his breathing had slowed, quiet snores escaping now and then. I stayed with him, not wanting to let go, and knew right then that I had to learn more about Lucy. I couldn't get lost in the moment and forget. If I were hallucinating, I needed to know. I needed to make sure I wasn't turning into Eddie.

11

Summer

I sat at the same table where Aaron had walked out on me the previous day. I faced the window this time, wanting to see him coming. The hangover had stuck with me for a second day. Not as bad, but the greasy aroma of the cafe did not do me any favours. There were no builders. Two men sat on the opposite side of the cafe. They spoke in whispers, for which my delicate head was grateful. I felt out of sorts. Like I was not actually in the cafe, but was watching from somewhere else.

I'd dressed in tight jeans and a yellow top which showed off my cleavage a bit. I'd even worn some light makeup. A part of me wanted Aaron to think I looked good. But mainly, I wanted to feel confident and in control. The makeup was like a mask of confidence. I wanted to be prepared to demand the truth. Anxiety still sat like a heavy knot in my stomach at the thought of what Aaron had to say. It must be about what happened to Lucy. Or that there was no Lucy, and I needed professional help.

I had dropped Joshua off at my mum's house an hour before.

Despite us not having a close relationship, she loved having him, and he loved being there. They adored each other. Mum was different these days, and she was great with him. She was a stereotypical grandma, or *Mamma*, as Joshua called her. He could do whatever he wanted when she was around and eat all the treats in her cupboard. Joshua got on better with her than I did, but then he didn't know what she was like after my dad died. He didn't know about the drinking. Nor would he, as long as she stayed off it. So there was no rush for me to get back to him, but I was not going to admit that to Aaron. Kids are a great excuse to get out of any situation, and one which I often used to its full advantage. After all, there had to be some perks to being a single mum.

I saw Aaron before he entered the cafe, as I'd hoped. His head was lowered, his shoulders pulled upwards to his ears, and his hands in the pockets of his black parka. I guessed he was attempting to keep the weak, but freezing, wind at bay. My heart surprised me with an involuntary flip that I immediately ignored. There was no way I was getting close to anyone after my last shit show of a *relationship* with Richard. The last couple of days didn't fill me with confidence in Aaron being a reliable and trustworthy partner either.

The bell above the front door jingled as he pushed it open and took one enormous step inside with his long legs. He closed the door behind him immediately. I liked that gesture. Most people would think nothing of closing the door quickly. But to me, it showed empathy for those around him. Of course, it may also be that he was cold. But then, my habit of overthinking human behaviour was likely another reason I enjoyed studying psychology so much.

Once over the threshold, he lifted his head and searched the cafe, his expression serious. It didn't take long for his eyes to land on me. As soon as they did, he smiled anxiously. I returned his smile with a confident one, hoping to make him feel more comfortable. I needed to ensure he didn't back out of whatever he wanted to tell me. I wanted the truth about Lucy, and then I could move on. I could be with Joshua and carry on, making sure he was happy and safe. He was my priority. Everything else was background noise.

We greeted each other as he took the chair opposite to me, sprawling his elbows and arms out on the table once seated. He almost reached for me, but wasn't brave enough. I didn't bother making this any easier for him.

"Are you okay?" I asked, still smiling but with a lift of my eyebrows.

A part of me didn't care. The same part of me that wanted to run away and forget all about Lucy. It's anxiety, I told myself. I felt like my and Joshua's lives were on pause until I found out the truth about Lucy.

"Yes." He sounded surprised, as though he had no reason not to be okay. I raised my eyebrows even further, and he stopped smiling. "Well...I wanted to talk to you about something."

I waited, but he didn't continue. His mouth was half-open, but the words wouldn't come out.

"Go on," I encouraged him.

He smiled again and cleared his throat, but still he said nothing.

"I assume it's about Lucy?" I tried again.

"You're obsessed!" he retorted, snorting with laughter.

I threw him an annoyed look, and his expression sobered. "No, it's not about Lucy. It is about a girl, though."

"Oh God, you have a girlfriend?" I asked probably too loudly, but the suspicion angered me. I knew all too well the damage cheating could cause.

"No! Jeez, shhhhhh!" He spat the words at me and looked around. The couple at the other table glanced over but went back to their conversation when Aaron caught them looking.

"It's my ex-girlfriend. I'm having issues with her."

"Oh." I relaxed and considered him for a moment. I was unsure why he was offloading this on to me. I didn't care. Well, not enough to meet in person to discuss that, anyway. I said nothing further, and glared at him until he continued.

"Erm…I'm not sure how to say this, but she has issues. She's a bit of a nutter, to be honest. I didn't meet her at work, mind you!" He laughed at his grim joke. My glare intensified. His use of the word *nutter* had not helped my irritation towards him. "Erm…I think she's following me."

At first, I still didn't see why he'd brought me here. Then it dawned on me.

"Oh shit, the other night? She saw you come to mine?" I asked.

"Well, I don't know." He looked apologetic.

I didn't feel sympathy for him. Why the hell had he come back to mine if he had a potentially dangerous stalker?

"I saw her earlier on in the night, but that was before I saw you. I'm pretty sure I had lost her by then."

"Jesus, Aaron, what do you mean by nutter? Dangerous? Violent? Still in love with you?" My voice was still way too loud, but I didn't care. Let the others look if they wanted.

"Well, she has attacked people before, but I don't think she knows about you. She did *not* follow me here today. I made sure."

His revelation took me by surprise. Of all the things I had

imagined he might tell me, this was not one of them. I disliked being on the spot with no conversation prepared.

"Attacked who? Have you called the police?" I asked, not knowing what else to say.

"No, no. No need for that. She hasn't hurt anyone recently. Not since we split. She won't leave me alone. I'm sure she will give up soon. It's only been a couple of weeks."

I studied his face carefully. He looked agitated, troubled. That didn't mean he was lying, I supposed. I would probably look the same if I had a *nutter* for a stalker. But something felt off to me. Maybe this was his way of making sure I didn't want to see him anymore, but then that seemed extreme. Why not ghost me if that was what he wanted?

"If she doesn't know about me, then I'm not sure why you're telling me this," I said. I kept watching his expression for evidence of lying.

"Well, it was just in case, really. In case I'm wrong, and she *did* see us. I wanted you to be aware, I guess, what with having Joshua and all."

I stewed over his words for a moment. The nagging feeling that had bothered me since Friday intensified. One of my greatest fears was someone breaking into my home and me being unable to defend Joshua. And now there's a chance it might happen, thanks to Aaron. I didn't want to go home, and I certainly did not want Joshua there right now. I made a mental note to call my mum once I was finished with Aaron. I needed an excuse for Joshua to stay at hers for a night or two until I could make sure we were safe. Maybe I could say I found a rat.

"You could have told me this on the phone." My usually calm voice had a clearly annoyed undertone that I struggled to hide.

"Well, I wanted to make sure she wasn't near you. Can I come back to yours? I can make sure you're safe. As I said, it's just in case. I don't think she knows, and she definitely did not follow me here. I'd swear on my own life. Can I please hang around with you, to make sure she isn't about? I don't want anything to happen to you."

"Maybe you should have thought about that before." I couldn't help but retort.

I tried to think about whether I wanted Aaron with me. I didn't. But I supposed I'd be safer with him around if someone were to follow or attack me. I had been in a fight-or-flight situation before, and I'd done neither. I froze. My legs turned to jelly and wouldn't work. Like in the dream with Lucy, I couldn't move, never mind run or fight back. If it were Joshua in danger, I knew I would fight like hell. I had no doubt I would kill for him in an instant. But if it was me in trouble, well, I already knew I was useless. If Aaron's ex wanted him, it was surely safer not to be around him.

"Please, Summer." His eyes stared deep into mine.

"Look, I get you want to make sure I'm okay. But I'll be fine. I think you need to stay away."

"Well, can I at least call you later?" He looked like a kicked puppy.

"Okay." I agreed. "I need to get Joshua, anyway."

"Okay, I'll walk you out."

We left the cafe together. I tried not to look at the men who had clearly heard snippets of our conversation. Aaron followed behind me, wary of my prickly vibe. He was good at reading people, too.

The cold air nipped at my bare face as the cafe door closed behind us. The glare of sunlight bouncing off the roofs of nearby cars momentarily blinded me, but didn't do much to warm the air. I stood still for a moment and took in the fresh air. My nauseous stomach was much happier away from the greasy stench of the cafe. A strange feeling washed over me, though. I shifted uncomfortably, feeling as if someone was watching me. I glanced at Aaron, but he was looking at the ground again, still standing behind me. It was nothing. I was feeling paranoid after Aaron's revelation about his ex.

I chanced a scan across the road, and fear hit me in the stomach like a freight train. A dark figure stared at me from across the road, a figure with bright green eyes.

12

Summer

I turned to Aaron. I couldn't speak, but he felt my stare and looked up. My horror must have been obvious, judging from the worry on his face. No words came to me. I looked back towards Lucy, but she was gone. The street was empty. Some parked cars and a lamppost lined the street, but Lucy was nowhere to be seen. *Had she run away? Was she hiding somewhere?*

Aaron followed my gaze and looked across the road. I turned again to look at him, not sure what to say or do. His skin turned pale. He gulped. He knew what I had seen. It was written all over his face.

"Lucy was there!" I finally gasped, pointing over to where I had seen her.

He didn't look surprised, or like he thought I was crazy. He looked scared. I didn't know what he was about to say, but I could tell he believed me.

"Lucy?" He gathered himself back together and attempted another snort of laughter. He relented when he saw my serious face staring at him.

"Come on, let's get you home." He said with more sincerity.

"No, Aaron, she was there!" I had lost my calm exterior yet again.

"Okay," he said simply, taking my hand. It shivered, and he held it tighter.

I allowed him to lead me home. I kept checking behind us, across the road, down side streets, looking for Lucy, but she was nowhere. I still couldn't think straight when we reached my building a few minutes later. My mind was a fog of swirling thoughts as I tried to unlock the main door. Aaron took my keys from me and led me upstairs. We hadn't spoken a word to each other the entire way home. He led me inside the flat and straight to my couch.

"Let me make you some tea," he said.

I said nothing, and he disappeared into the kitchen. I could hear cupboard doors open and close again and again as he tried to find his way around. I didn't actually drink tea, but I did have tea bags hidden somewhere for the rare occasion we had a guest. It occurred to me I should help him, but I didn't move.

I took the steaming mug from him upon his return. The warmth of the cup felt good against my chilled fingers, if nothing else. Aaron sat beside me and put his hand on my leg. I didn't push it away.

"Did you see her?" I asked him.

He shook his head. "Babe…what exactly did you see?" he asked.

"It was her!" I pulled my leg away from his hand and scowled at him.

"Did you see her face?" he asked.

He appeared genuinely curious as to what I had seen rather

than disbelieving. At least he didn't accuse me of seeing things. Which, to me, was more evidence that he knew Lucy was real. I thought about how to answer his question.

"Well, yes…I think so." I frowned and thought about it some more. I knew I'd seen a female figure with dark hair, a large coat, and dark trousers. But no. I hadn't seen her face clearly. Not at all, honestly.

But I knew it was her. Like when you see a friend in a random place and you *know* it's them without seeing their face. Except Lucy wasn't a friend.

"I'm not sure," I admitted. Tiredness overtook me and I hid my head in my hands.

He placed his large hand back on my leg and squeezed. I put my hand on his and looked into his eyes, searching for signs of dishonesty as he spoke.

"I believe you." He looked so sincere I wondered if he was about to admit to something. "I believe you think you saw Lucy, but I also believe I freaked you out with all my bullshit about my ex. Think about it. I tell you some girl might be following me, then we walk outside and you see a girl looking at us? Obviously, you still have Lucy on your mind, so you're going to assume it is her, but babe, *think*. Have you seen Lucy at any other time, other than that horrible dream?"

I shook my head. I supposed he was right. I hadn't seen Lucy at all since my nightmare. The timing was suspect too. Maybe I was jumpy, and my mind was seeing things. Or maybe it was some random person.

"And if she was there, if it was Lucy, why would she be following you? And where did she go?" He pressed further.

I shrugged my shoulders. I had no answers, still only questions, but Aaron knew about Lucy. If she was following me, then Joshua and I weren't safe. I knew what I had to do.

"I'm going to ask my mum to keep Joshua for the night," I told Aaron. I looked up at him. "Will you stay with me tonight?"

"Of course," he nodded, "whatever you need. Go to your mum's and see Joshua. I'll go to the shop for some drinks and come back here when you're ready." He winked at me, and I managed a smile. "Then you and I are going to chill out and watch a movie together."

I ached for Joshua to come home, not Aaron. But I had to make sure we were safe. I had to get the truth out of Aaron.

13

Summer

I allowed Aaron to guide me outside to my car, and dropped him off at the supermarket on the way to my mum's. She lived twenty minutes away in the old mining town of Ilkeston, near Richard. I arrived at her two-bed semi feeling better, though still not myself. I pulled up on the street outside, ignoring her empty driveway. I liked to have a quick escape from the awkwardness of our stilted relationship. I checked the mirror, my pale face looking back at me despite the smattering of makeup I'd applied earlier that day. I tried to neaten my windswept hair by running my fingers through it but gave up and closed the mirror.

I pulled my coat tighter and made my way up the tarmac driveway. I knocked on Mum's door and waited for her to open it as a stranger would. We were close too when I was Joshua's age, but it all went wrong after my dad's death. At ten years old, I'd been devastated and in desperate need of her guidance. Mum was devastated and turned to alcohol for her guidance. It terrified me that Joshua and I might someday grow apart. I couldn't imagine it. I would do anything in my power to ensure we didn't end up little more than strangers. It didn't take long for Mum to come to the door. She smiled but held her head down rather than look me in the eye. I gave her a tight smile back. I could hear Joshua's shouts the second I entered the tiny grey entrance hall.

"Mummy!" he yelled. I dodged Mum's tired-looking shoe cabinet and coat stand, entering the living room through the open door.

I don't think I'd ever squeezed Joshua so hard. He moaned at me for hurting his sides, but I wanted so badly never to let go and bring him home with me. He fit so perfectly in my arms, he always had done no matter how much he grew. I reminded myself repeatedly that I was leaving him there for a good reason.

"Are you okay, Mummy?" He looked at me quizzically. He knew me better than anyone, despite his young age, and could always tell when something was wrong. No matter how hard I tried to hide it. He worried about me far too much. It was as if he thought he needed to take care of me rather than the other way around.

"Yes! Just sad that you can't come home, baby." I kissed him again. He seemed to believe me and gave me another tight squeeze.

"It makes me sad too." His bottom lip stuck out as he looked up at me with big eyes.

My stomach flip-flopped as guilt tore at me. I should never have gotten involved with Lucy's disappearance. I should have believed Aaron and moved on with my life.

We played games for a bit on his tablet before I put Joshua to bed in my mum's spare room. I bought him a new audiobook on my phone, and we listened to it for a while. We giggled together at the silly story of a naughty boy who liked to cheat. I lay with him until I heard quiet snores. I stayed a little longer in case he woke, and then snuck out. Downstairs my mum was sitting on her red recliner watching the news, her glasses perched on the end of her nose. The decade of alcohol abuse was visible in her aged skin and lack of teeth. She had lost a lot of weight since she stopped drinking and looked far more fragile. Another pang of guilt grabbed at me. She had been through more than most people.

"Hi, Mum." My words were always stilted around her. I wished they weren't, but I couldn't help it. There were too many unspoken words between us.

She smiled up at me. "Is he asleep?" she asked. Wisps of her shoulder-length grey hair fell around her hollow cheeks. I nodded. "I would have been happy to lie with him, you know. He's such a Mummy's boy."

I tried not to let my irritation show. What does it matter if he's a Mummy's boy?

"Well, yeah, we're close," I stated simply. "I'm going to go to the shop to see if I can get anything to sort out the rat."

"You'll need a proper store, not the supermarket. Why don't you stay here too? For one night."

If someone had told me last week that I would consider sleeping at my mum's house, I would've laughed in their face. But as I looked at the fragile old lady, watching the telly alone, I felt a need to sit with her. I realised I felt safer here than in my flat. I considered my options. If I was to stay here, then we'd both be safe. For tonight at least. It would be short term, though. To make sure we were safe forever, I needed to speak to Aaron. I needed to find out what he wasn't telling me.

So instead, I said a rushed goodbye to my mum. We were

closer than we used to be, thanks to Joshua. But I still didn't hug and kiss her or tell her I loved her. We weren't there yet, so instead, I threw a graceless wave her way before I walked away.

Back in the car, I felt stronger now that I had some semblance of a plan and finally felt a sense of calm. Seeing Joshua's sad face had given me new strength, and no matter what was happening with Lucy, I needed to stop it. I needed to make sure Joshua was safe. I needed to find her before she found me again.

14

For You...

I had a good view of them both through the window. Though I had to be careful that she didn't spot me. It didn't matter if Aaron saw me, he wouldn't tell. But it wasn't time for her to see me yet. She had her tits on show for him, which didn't surprise me. She even wore makeup. Not that it made her look any better, she may as well not have bothered. She won't be able to wear it when I'm done with her, anyway.

I was pleased to see that she didn't look too happy. Her brow furrowed as she looked at him, but I couldn't tell from this distance if it was anger or disappointment. I wondered what they were discussing to make her feel that way. It better not be me. *No.* I laughed the thought away. Aaron wouldn't be that stupid.

I was still reeling from my earlier discovery. Summer had a child, a young boy. He was the image of her with the same brown hair and light eyes. He had darker skin, though. Despite looking like her, the boy was beautiful. I had heard her shout his name when he ran too far ahead to the car. *Joshua.* I knew the second I saw him that I was going to have him. He would be mine, and I would love him and cherish him far more than *her*. I'd share him with no one, and she would have no one. Loneliness could be her punishment. It was far better than simply making her ugly. She'd made me lonely, she'd taken my home, so I would make her lonely and take her home. I would take her boy.

I would still make her ugly as well, though. I needed to have some fun. Plus, that way, she wouldn't be able to look after anyone when I was done with her. She would be ugly, and everyone would stare, but not because they wanted her. No one would want her. Joshua wouldn't want her. Aaron wouldn't want her.

She would be completely alone. They won't even notice when she doesn't return home. No one would want her.

15

Summer

I picked Aaron up from his flat on my way back and apologised for taking so long. He didn't seem to mind. He was much perkier than when I had left him in the supermarket, and I was feeling much better myself, thanks to my plan. He had two bottles of white wine in his bag, along with some vodka and a bottle of lemonade. I was certainly not planning on drinking that much, but I wondered how much alcohol it would take to get him to open up about Lucy. I was feeling confident I was going to get the truth. When we arrived back at my flat, I poured each of us a large glass of wine.

"How about we watch a film?" Aaron asked.

I agreed. I'd get him talking eventually, and a film was the perfect opportunity for him to get some alcohol down. I let him choose the movie, and he picked a comedy with Eddie Murphy. I took small sips of my wine and went to the toilet shortly after to pour the rest of the glass down the sink.

"I'm going for a top-up," I told Aaron. "Do you want one?"

"Sure," Aaron replied. I felt guilty as he smiled at me, but then I thought of Joshua, and the feeling dissipated.

By the time the film finished, both bottles of wine were gone. Aaron was smiley and chatty. His hand had made its way to my leg, and he was feeling braver. I moved closer to him, and he turned to face me. I smiled at him, inviting him to come closer. He moved forward, and his rough stubble gently grazed my face as we kissed. His touch was light at first but quickly deepened as our hunger for each other grew.

I felt his fingers graze my hip as he slowly manoeuvred his hand beneath my top. His cold fingertips tickled my stomach as he reached for my breasts.

I pulled my mouth away. "Wait. We need to talk, Aaron."

He carried on kissing my neck, his stubble digging into my skin. I couldn't help the moan that escaped my lips as he moved his hand back down over my stomach. I had to be cautious not to scare him off. I needed him to know he could open up to me and tell me the truth. But as his hand slipped into my trousers, I didn't want him to stop. He inserted a finger deep inside me, and my moans became louder.

Lucy's face flashed in mind, invading the space between us. I pushed him up so I could wiggle away.

"Aaron, I know you're not telling me something," I blurted out. *Shit.*

He sat back with a disappointed look on his face. "I thought you were enjoying it," he said.

"I was." I smiled at him, and he leaned towards me.

"Then let me carry on," he said with a smirk.

"I want to know about Lucy first. I need to get her out of my head. I can't relax."

He sighed and sat back. "Okay, but you're going to think I'm crazy," he replied.

A tremendous sense of relief washed over me. He was finally going to tell me the truth.

I laughed. "I won't!" I said. "I need to know that I'm not crazy."

"Okay, look, there *was* a Lucy Clarke who stayed on Bluebell Ward, but... she doesn't stay there anymore." Aaron looked pointedly at me.

"Okay. So she's moved on? Why lie about it?" I asked.

"No, I haven't told you everything yet." He sighed and looked down at his knees.

"Aaron, tell me, please."

"She died, Summer."

I heard his words, but I didn't understand. "I spoke to her a couple of hours before I spoke to you and asked if she was poorly. I'm pretty sure I would have noticed if a patient died whilst I was on the ward! And again, why would you lie about it?"

He was quiet for a moment before finally replying. "No, I mean, she died a long time ago. Before I was even working on the ward, it must have been about ten years ago."

Shock vibrated through me like an electrical current. Of all the things I thought Aaron might tell me, Lucy being a ghost, was not one of them.

"So I've been seeing a ghost?" I laughed quietly at first, but within a few seconds, I was verging hysterical. I couldn't help it. I thought about her cold lank fingers on my arm and the way she had drifted towards me whilst I lay in bed. My laughter stopped, and Aaron stared at me, full of concern.

"I don't know what you've seen," he said and shrugged his shoulders.

"It can't have been a ghost! She talked to me in front of

others. She must have!"

"I don't know what to say." He looked at me, more dismal than I'd ever seen him.

I examined what he'd told me. *Lucy* and *Clarke* are both common names. It's possible another Lucy Clarke had been on the ward years ago.

"What happened to the Lucy Clarke you're talking about?" I asked him.

"Well, apparently she had paranoid schizophrenia, and she was in on a section 37/41. She had voices in her head, they told her to be violent."

"A section 37/41? What crime did she commit then?" I asked. Patients convicted of a crime could be detained under Section 37 by criminal courts. The additional Section 41 was included if the Crown Court thought the patient was a serious risk to the public.

"Something about stalking that got out of hand." He shrugged his shoulders, and looked away again. There was a wistful look in his eyes. He probably wanted to be anywhere else but with me. "I know some patients talk about her, so I asked Emma, and that's what she said. The patients think they see her too. I've thought I've seen her once or twice, Summer." He looked back at me. "Once on the ward, and outside once, too. Hence why I freak out whenever you think you see her."

"Well, what happened to her in the end? Did she leave the ward?" I asked.

"She died in a fire."

My stomach flipped upside down and I closed my eyes, trying to steady myself. I knew there had been a fire at Bluebell Ward because of a plaque that was stuck to the wall in the corridor. It listed the names of patients who had died in that fire. Was the name Lucy Clarke on it? I couldn't remember, but I'd never read the names in any great detail. I opened my eyes.

"I think you should go. It's late," I told Aaron.

"Really?" He looked disappointed. "I was hoping I could stay and make you feel safe."

"I'm fine. I do feel safe," I lied. I'd feel safer without him.

"Okay, if you're sure." He placed his empty glass down on the coffee table and stood up to leave. "Bye." He stood awkwardly with his hands in his pockets.

"Bye." I got up to walk him out. I smiled at him but stayed a few steps back. I didn't want him to touch me, and I wanted to make that clear.

He looked solemn as he left, but as harsh as it sounded, I didn't care. He'd lied to me again. I needed a new plan.

16

Summer

I sat in my living room after Aaron had left. His story made no sense to me. I refused to believe I was speaking to a ghost the whole time on the ward. I would have known. Other people would have seen her, or I would have looked like I was talking to myself.

Lucy had touched me. She'd grabbed my arm on more than one occasion, brushed her fingers through my hair. I shivered remembering how cold her hands were. I didn't understand why Aaron had fed me such a ridiculous story. There was fear in his voice as he spoke about her that made me wonder if he believed it. Maybe someone had told him. He'd said Emma had said it, but she didn't strike me as the kind to believe in patient ghost stories.

I wasn't even sure if *I* believed in ghosts. My nana had a ghost in her bungalow, according to my mum. I couldn't remember my nana as she died when I was six. She and Mum were not close. But when I was small, Mum would tell me tales of a ghost who watched her and her three siblings in the bedroom. Things would move on their own, and in the dead of night, they could hear heavy breathing. I'd thought she was making it up. I'd never seen a ghost before or heard of any concrete evidence.

I thought of my older brother Eddie, and tried to remember the last time I saw him. It was a few months after Dad died. He was twenty then. It was eighteen years ago, yet I remembered the violence as though it were yesterday. How he had threatened Mum as I hid. How Marinda had tried to stop him. His hallucinations were no longer auditory. The devil was following him everywhere he went, and he had to do what the devil said.

I am not my brother. I am not my brother. I am not ill.

My laptop sat on the dining table, so I meandered over to review my diary entries once again. I tried to remember every time Lucy and I had spoken as the old laptop kicked into gear. I couldn't remember seeing her speak to any other patients. That wasn't unusual for the people living on the wards I visited, because they mainly consisted of severe personality disorder patients. It was a wide spectrum of possible illnesses. It was common for people to keep to themselves, and I didn't blame them. People who suffer from poor mental health are more likely to be victims than perpetrators of a violent attack. But every ward I visited had some particularly violent patients living there. It was a high-stress environment, and the patients were already burdened by mental health. These were not people I would want to live with whilst trying to work through my own problems. I often wondered how forcing ill people together helped them to overcome their issues. I could guarantee that being forced to live in such a place would drive me completely over the edge.

But there must have been at least one time Lucy spoke to

someone else. I remembered her threatening aura, the stench of cigarettes, and the shiny grease that coated her hair. She was solid. I shook my head. Ghosts weren't like that. *Were they?* Then there's Aaron, but I clearly wasn't getting the truth out of him. Whatever the truth might be, he was hiding it from me. I opened up the files on my laptop and started scrolling through notes again. One, in particular, jumped out at me, and I realised what I'd been missing. *How could I have forgotten?*

I'd had my evidence that Aaron knew Lucy all along. I grabbed my phone and brought up Aaron's number. He answered on the second ring.

"Hey, Summer. Good timing. I just reached my flat. Are you okay?"

"No, Aaron, I'm not okay. You're lying to me, and I know it now." I listened for his reaction. My words were met with silence, so I continued. "Lucy fell out with me a few weeks ago. She went mad and thought I'd been telling lies to the staff about her. She thought I was responsible for her ward round being cancelled. You and Emma had to restrain her." I left my revelation hanging in the air. I could hear him breathing, but nothing else.

"I don't remember," Aaron replied. His voice was hesitant.

"You're lying to me." I couldn't be bothered to argue with him. "And I'm going to find out why."

17

Aaron

Aaron's phone made a thud as it fell from his hand. His legs gave way, and he dropped to the floor with his head in his hands. He felt panic rise as he tried to figure out what to do next. Giving up was what he *wanted* to do. Maybe he should tell the truth. His crazy ex-girlfriend lie hadn't worked, but he had hoped the story about Lucy's death would scare Summer off. Clearly not. He needed to get her off the scent somehow before she got hurt. But now she didn't trust him, and he was running out of options.

He lowered his hands and raised his head. Hot tears ran down his cheeks, wet circles appearing on his jeans as his tears dropped. He needed help, but he couldn't go to the police. There was one person he knew that might be able to help him, but calling them would be dangerous. He wasn't even sure if he had kept their phone number.

Aaron ignored the ache in his legs as he pushed himself up off the ground. He stalked over to the open kitchen and frantically searched the drawers, looking for the tiny scrap of paper that had recently been pushed through his letterbox.

But it was nowhere in sight. He moved into his bedroom and rummaged through the bedside cabinet. Again, he found nothing. He racked his brain, trying to remember where he had put the note as he walked back into the kitchen. His eyes fell on the bin. He remembered scrunching up the paper and throwing it away. He hadn't wanted it then. The risk was too great.

Now, it was the one thing that could help him, Summer, and Joshua. He had seen a picture of Joshua on Summer's bedside table. The boy had the same light brown hair, beautiful big blue eyes, and freckle-spattered nose as Summer. He had even fantasised about meeting Joshua despite Summer and him only recently sleeping together for the first time. Aaron couldn't believe his luck when she'd walked onto the ward a few months ago. She was way out of his league, though. He'd always been too shy to say anything to her. But now he could have his own ready-made family and maybe even add another child. His mother would love Summer. She had far more class than any other girl he had brought home.

Holding his breath, he opened the bin and carefully took out the top layer of rubbish and threw it on the floor beside him. Eventually, he saw the note beneath a piece of tin foil. It was stained orange with what looked like bean juice. He gingerly took it out and wiped it down with a kitchen towel. He could have kissed it if it weren't covered in God knows how many germs. The note in front of him had a name and a phone number written in a sprawling, child-like handwriting. The name was Lucy.

18

Summer

I'd spent the entire night on the sofa, drifting in and out of sleep. Lucy visited my dreams, but it wasn't as realistic as the previous nightmare. It was Monday and I was due back on Bluebell Ward that morning. I forced myself to get off the sofa and take a shower. My hair was getting so long that it was a pain to blow dry, but I took the time to wash and dry it, anyway. It desperately needed a good trim, but I hated going to the hairdressers. All the physical contact and small talk meant I'd sit in the chair, itching to leave.

I threw on some black suit trousers and a pretty cream blouse. I chose a black cardigan which was smart but not lawyer-like. It was important to be smart but approachable. I couldn't look intimidating like a lawyer.

A part of me didn't want to go back to Bluebell Ward. I wasn't sure why, as Lucy obviously wasn't there. But I knew I needed to get her file. Aaron had told me during the previous night's film that he was not on shift today. I hadn't heard from him since I hung up the phone. I'd meant every word about finding the truth, and knew what I had to do. I rang Joshua before I left. We spoke for a few minutes, and I told him to be good for his mamma and get ready for school. I felt calmer after our chat, but my head began to pound when I started driving. A heavy cloud of dread surrounded me as I pulled into the hospital car park, making my headache feel even worse.

I forced a few deep breaths in through the nose and out through the mouth before pushing myself out of the deep front seat of the BMW. Despite my forced breathing, the cloud of dread grew heavier as I walked through the doors of the reception area. I needed to sign in with the receptionist and get my ward keys.

Though they made me feel like a jailer from an old prison movie walking around with twenty-odd keys swinging off his pockets. Once I had them and had placed my coat, handbag, and laptop into the reception room locker, I entered the first of many corridors to get to Bluebell Ward.

Every secure hospital I visited was a maze of locked corridors. It took time to learn the correct way around the building with each one. Staff left me to it. They were worried that if they helped me, they might say something that would get them in trouble with the advocate. Not wanting to appear panicked, and be mistaken for one of the ward's patients, I tried my quiet, deep breathing all the way, but it didn't help. The anxiety wouldn't leave me. I kept expecting Lucy to jump out of a wall or something equally ridiculous. I walked through the winding, tiled corridors, unlocking what felt like a million doors as I went. By the time I'd reached the Bluebell ward entrance, my apprehension was suffocating me.

I stopped still, unable to raise the keys. Instead, I stood in front of the doors, looking through the glass panel to the corridor on the other side. The same corridor where I last saw

Lucy. *I didn't have to go in there. I could quit my job, move house, move Joshua's school...*

I realised that was ridiculous. I didn't have the savings needed to move house. Although, if I did, I'm pretty sure I would have chosen the simple way out to protect us. Again, I half expected to see Lucy as my eyes searched the corridor through the panel, but Louise stood there alone, leaning back with one foot against the wall, her head down. She must have been able to feel my gaze because she raised her head and looked straight at me. Her eyes widened. She didn't smile, but she was clearly eager to see me. *Shit*. I had to go in.

With my rising anxiety attempting to suffocate me, I forced my hand to open the door. I had to be quick and alert around patients for fear they would try to escape. None had ever managed it in this manner to my knowledge, at least not recently, but it was drilled into all staff to know that it could happen.

I wasn't moving fast. My legs felt like jelly and were difficult to move. I looked at Louise as I entered and forced a smile before slowly turning my back on her to lock the door. Another thing I shouldn't do ideally, but Louise wasn't much of a risk to me. Like most patients, she was more of a risk to herself than anyone else.

"Can we talk?" Louise asked without saying hello. She clearly had no time for manners, but that was okay. The women on this ward usually had far bigger things to worry about than good manners. Plus, it took much more than that to offend me. Like multiple lies from someone I'd slept with.

"Sure, see you in the room in two minutes?" I asked. I needed to let the ward staff know I was there and would be alone with Louise in the room.

The room I referred to was a private space on the ward where patients or staff could have meetings without leaving the secure area. This was only allowed with certain patients who did not have a history of violence towards staff, like Louise. It was a room I was familiar with, a claustrophobic space with no window. All four walls were whitewashed, turning grey with age. A round wooden table sat in the corner with some chairs gathered around, and a white bench lined the far wall. It wasn't an easy room to be in if you were already struggling to breathe.

I walked over to the nurses' station and let them know I was on the ward and going to the private room with Louise. They were friendly enough and confirmed it was safe to go into the room alone with Louise. They warned me about a couple of patients who had shown aggression already and let me on my way. I looked around the ward. It was quiet that morning. A lot of patients were on medications that made them docile, so it was not unusual for them to sleep in. It was barely 10 AM after all, and they had nowhere to be. There were two patients in the communal living area, and both were draped over the sofas with their eyes closed. The TV quietly showed an episode of some daytime talk show. The smell of porridge hung thick in the air.

I entered the meeting room, still a bit unstable on my legs but moving easier than before. Being on the ward was not as bad as I'd thought, everything seemed so *normal*. Louise was waiting for me. She seemed okay, if maybe nervous. She jumped right in, speaking about her ward round meeting. She was going to be first today. The meeting was at 10:30, and she wanted section 17 leave. I didn't blame her. The hospital gave all patients the same deal when they first arrived. They could not leave the ward until their behaviour and mood had been assessed by staff. Eventually, with good behaviour, the patient would be allowed to go out by themselves. If anything untoward happened, or they did not return by a certain time, one hour a week at first, then two hours, then three, etc., their privilege would be revoked, and they would have to go back to the beginning to build it up again.

Louise was allowed out with a staff member for two hours every alternate day. She wanted her leave to be alone now and needed me to attend the ward round in case she got too nervous to ask. I forced my own feelings aside and agreed to help. We moved back into the communal area and talked until one of the support workers smiled at Louise and shouted her name. The support staff could get super friendly with the patients, although they had to be careful not to let their guard down. I'd seen violent attacks happen to staff and had been threatened myself on a couple of occasions. Most recently was the Lucy incident. The one that Aaron *did not remember*.

I walked next to Louise as we left the ward with the support worker. We made our way down one of the winding corridors, through three air-locked doors, and into a conference room. It was a stark contrast from the patients' tiny meeting room on the ward. It was sunny and cheerful, with a large, oval table taking up the middle of the room. A crisp breeze came in through the open window, making the room cool.

There were already a few people sitting around the table, all looking at Louise, smiling, and saying hello. Some smiled at me, too. Some ignored me, unsure how to act around me. These people made up the multidisciplinary team, or the MDT, at the hospital. The team consisted of the lead nurse from the ward, Emma Fahy, the consultant psychologist, the art therapist, social worker, occupational therapist, and key support worker. It was no wonder patients felt intimidated in such meetings with all of these authorities around them. I knew I would be daunted if they were discussing me, and that was without being mentally fragile.

I took a seat next to Louise and looked around at the people in front of me. A moment of clarity ran through me as if someone had turned on a light in my fog-addled brain. I realised who could help me.

Everyone sitting here should know about Lucy. *But who would tell me?* I had to be careful. I was there to support patients, but the hospital was my employer's customer. The hospital paid for our advocacy service. Therefore, although most staff didn't realise it and patients certainly did not know, I could not annoy or upset the staff. If they complained about me, my employer could replace me, or the hospital might cancel their contract. It was a dynamic I'd always hated. Not all advocacy services worked this way, but the private ones did.

As Louise and I took our seats, the lead psychiatrist, Dr Rears, entered the room. His colossal frame took up most of the doorway, despite being stooped from age. I wondered if he was past retirement age. He must have been at least pushing it. The quicker he retired, the better. He smiled at us all from under his fluffy white moustache. Dr Rears would tell you he does not drink alcohol, but his skin suggested otherwise. Like my mum's skin.

I had disliked Dr Rears since our first encounter, when he was training all staff on how to *deal* with the patients. There had been lots of *us* and *them* mentioned. I had secretly diagnosed him with Narcissistic Personality Disorder. I had voiced my concerns to Natalie once, but she dismissed them as usual.

His sly eyes lingered on Emma as he took his seat next to Louise. She didn't seem to notice. Her head was pointed down as she read the patient file in front of her. Her blonde hair fell in front of her face. Such behaviour was typical of Dr Rears and made my stomach churn, but my detest came from somewhere deeper. Ever the professional, I smiled and greeted Dr Rears as usual. He did not appear pleased to see me. The psychiatrists never were. Advocates got in their way. I imagined having an advocate in the ward round was like the dynamic of having a new boss watch you while you work. It would be dangerous to do anything too stupid in front of me.

The meeting began with Dr Rears asking Louise how she was, what she had been up to. Had she been feeling positive and sleeping well? Louise responded optimistically, trying hard to remain calm and give off a confident aura. Dr Rears then spoke to each staff member in turn, asking for an update whilst Louise looked on. I could never imagine how difficult it must be to have these professionals in charge of your life. Everything being scrutinised under their watch and right in front of you. Luckily for Louise, all were positive for the day. Dr Rears asked her if she had anything further to say, and she looked at me. Her large brown eyes were full of anxiety and fear of rejection. I heeded her sign.

"Louise feels she has been making significant progress, and she would like to request unsupervised leave, please." I smiled at Louise and turned my attention back to Dr Rears, who answered Louise directly, as he should.

After considering the feedback, he confirmed that she could have two hours a week unsupervised. If it went well, she could look to increase it in thirty days. Louise beamed from ear to ear, clearly delighted.

Once the meeting was finished, I asked Dr Rears if I could have a word with him. He confirmed he would find me once ward rounds were completed for the day. I thanked him and left the room with Louise. She skipped back to the ward. I was smiling too, but my happiness was more to do with being one step closer to finding Lucy.

Dr Rears might disgust me, but he must have been Lucy's psychiatrist and, therefore, her responsible clinician. He must have known where she was. He couldn't lie about that.

19

Summer

Dr Rears did not come and find me after the final ward round had finished. So an hour after the last meeting, I went looking for him. I checked all the wards, the smoking area, and his office but eventually found him in the staff room drinking a cup of tea. He looked up as I entered, and his eyes widened when he saw me standing at the doorway.

"Oh, hi!" he exclaimed, throwing his hands up in an exaggerated expression of relief and standing up. "I'm glad you found me!"

He spoke as though he had been looking for me rather than hiding from me.

"Hi." I smiled and stepped closer to him despite my mind screaming at me to stay away from him. "You got a sec now?"

"Sure." He beamed from ear to ear and walked around to my side of the table so we were face to face. I resisted an urge to punch him in the mouth. "Which patient is it regarding, by the way?"

"It's a strange one. I'm looking for Lucy…" I trailed off to watch his expression. His face showed no reaction at first, but then his forehead wrinkled and his lips pursed.

"Lucy? Hm. I don't think she's one of mine? I don't have a Lucy. Which ward is she on?" He was a good liar. It clearly came easy to him.

"Bluebell. Lucy Clarke. In her twenties, lots of scar tissue on her face from burns. Section 37/41," I replied.

"Nope, I don't know of any Lucy Clarke, sorry." He shrugged his shoulders and stood up. "She must be in one of your other hospitals."

He left his tea on the table and dashed out of the kitchen before I could respond to his suggestion that I was confused. Him undermining my professionalism hadn't bothered me. It took much more than that to insult me. He had intrigued me further, though. He was also lying to me. I had no desire to follow him out of the kitchen. Now both Dr Rears and Aaron were lying to me. I had to think about who else I could turn to. I didn't want to speak to the patients for fear of scaring them. Most were paranoid enough without me making it worse.

I headed back to Bluebell ward and visited the nurses' station where the patient files were stored on the computer. Each patient had their own personal case file. It contained their background, childhood traumas, diagnoses, and notes of all of their care-related activity whilst in the hospital. The files fascinated me, though some were heartbreaking. I didn't automatically read every patient file, I only read them where necessary for my job. I was legally allowed access to any file as long as the patient gave me permission, but the ward staff never double-checked with the patient. They never even asked *me* if I had permission. They always left me to it. I'd never been sure if they didn't know I needed the patient's consent or they were too scared to ask me.

But then I was a professional. Why would I lie? Plus, too many staff didn't care about such rules. They liked the *nice* patients, the daytime outings and the money. Even the staff who cared about the patients didn't fully understand my role, and so they never questioned what I was doing on the computer. To be fair to them, I usually would never lie about something so serious. I could have lost my job. However, I needed to check for Lucy's file, and there was no chance of being caught, so there wasn't any real risk.

As I entered the ward again, the plaque on the wall caught my eye. I knew Aaron was lying about the fact he thought I'd been talking to a ghost, but I scanned my eyes over the plaque anyway, searching for Lucy's name. I was saddened to see that it was a long list. Each name had an age next to it. *Anna Bishop, aged 53. Rose McDonald, aged 42. Amber Vish, aged 19.* Annoyingly it was not in alphabetical order, and it wasn't until I reached the end of the list that I saw a name which made goosebumps rise over every inch of my skin. *Lucie Clarke, aged 25.*

20

Summer

I told myself it couldn't be her. Lucy Clarke was a common name. Plus, they'd spelled it differently. I was sure she spelled it *Lucy Clark* and not *Lucie Clarke*. And Lucie had been twenty-five. The Lucy I knew was older than me, at least in her forties. I racked my brain, trying to think where I'd seen her name written down other than how I imagined it to be spelled. Then I remembered the patient files. There must be answers in there if Lucy was real. Which she was. I knew she must be. I couldn't even consider the alternative. *I am not like my brother.*

I continued through the ward and let myself into the empty nurses' station. The staff were out on the ward by then. Most were watching TV with a few of the patients. My anxiety dissipated once I'd rationalised that it *must* be a different Lucy. I was invigorated with a newfound confidence. I didn't know what was going on, but I knew I was not crazy. Although I was acutely aware that anyone suffering from hallucinations would say the same.

I sat down at the desk and opened the password-protected

folder on the computer. I scanned through the list of names. As with most patient documents, they were all saved under initials for security. Most of which I recognised. Not all patients wanted to use an advocate. Some had great family support or enough confidence of their own. Some did not trust us. A lot of patients with such debilitating mental health had traumatic experiences with authority figures that resulted in them not trusting anyone, so it was no surprise. It wasn't my job to help them with such issues. That was what therapy and medication were for.

I soon lost hope as I flicked through the initials. There was one file named *LC*, but on closer inspection of the documents inside, I found it was for Isabelle, as Aaron had mentioned to me previously. As I was about to give up and log off, an unusual file caught my eye. It was at the bottom of the list of files and entitled *ZZ_AG_Duplicate*. I double-clicked into the file and, at first glance, it appeared to be another dead end. AG stood for Alison Gile. I'd spoken to her once or twice but didn't know her well. All the files inside the folder were entitled *AG:Therapy1* or *AG:Ward_round_week37*. It seemed like a duplicate of the original AG file. But nobody else had a duplicate file, so why did AG? I opened the file entitled *AG_Background*.

What I saw made me feel a way I had never experienced before, as if my heart had risen and sank simultaneously. I was nauseous yet so completely triumphant that I wanted to grab the nearest person and scream *I fucking told you so* in their face. There it was in glorious colour, a picture of Lucy. I couldn't believe it at first, but I zoomed in on the tiny photo, and there was no mistaking her scarred features and shocking green eyes. I began to read.

LC, aged 29, was committed to Bluebell Ward following a transfer from Havensfield Hospital in South London. LC was in Havensfield for 2 years and has been in different institutions since the age of 19, following the death of her infant son. It is believed LC caused the death of her son by drowning him in the kitchen sink when she was 19.

A shiver chilled my bones. I knew Lucy had somehow hurt her child. She had mentioned causing her child pain in previous conversations. However, I did not realise she had *murdered* her own baby. My stomach turned as I ordered myself to keep reading.

LC was removed from the care of her parents at the age of 10 following a report from a neighbour that she was being neglected. Following a visit from social services, LC was found to be living in squalid conditions and covered in suspicious looking injuries. These included severe bruising to the breast and thigh area and marks that looked like cigarette burns on her arms and legs. LC will not discuss this part of her childhood. She was sent to a foster home at age 10, where she stayed for 18 months before moving to another foster home due to violent outbursts. Her initial foster family reported her as being defiant, staying out all night, smashing ornaments in the house, and uncontrollable. She stayed at the second foster home from age 12 to 14, when she reportedly ran away and was never found. LC has informed us she was homeless and lived on the streets until the age of 16 when she moved in with a man. She will only refer to this man as 'Bainsy' and will not reveal his full name. She has said she had sex with his friends for money. She did not see this money, but in her words, Bainsy took care of her and bought her anything she needed. She got pregnant aged 18 and gave birth aged 19. She was still living with Bainsy but stated that she did not know who the father was. She will not discuss the death of the child, but police reports show that Bainsy found the dead child in the sink, and he started to beat Lucy. He tied LC to a chair and set the flat on fire, taking the infant with him. A neighbour called the fire brigade. Bainsy told the police it was LC who murdered the child. They saved LC from the fire but she suffered severe burns. LC did not speak a word to police and ended up being charged for the filicide but committed under a section 37/41.

Tears for Lucy and her baby stung my eyes as I read. She was clearly extremely vulnerable but also dangerous. There was no way I was letting her near Joshua no matter how much sympathy I had for her childhood. The sound of voices alerted me to a nurse walking towards the station. I pulled myself out of the black hole I had fallen into whilst reading Lucy's file. A curse escaped me as I realised I had no way of copying it for evidence or for further information. I snapped open the therapy contacts file, grabbed my phone and stole a picture of the names to check later. I shoved my phone back in my pocket and closed the file, smiling at the nurse as she entered the office. She smiled back.

"What are you up to?" she asked innocently enough, but concern heaved up from my stomach.

"Oh, looking into something for Louise," I replied, grinning like an idiot. "What about you?"

"Grabbing some phones." She picked up the mobile phones she was referring to and took a seat to record what she was doing. Some patients were allowed supervised phone access at certain times of the day. As I watched her, an idea came to me of who else might be able to help me.

"Is Emma around?" Surely Emma would know where Lucy was.

"She's off sick." The girl replied without looking up.

"Oh, I saw her this morning in Louise's ward round. She seemed fine."

"Yeah, she went off sick after ward rounds, not sure what's wrong with her."

I gave in and left the office to finish off on the ward. I made a plan to look at the contacts for Lucy later. I promised myself I was going to find her. I was going to catch her. And then, I was going to help her.

21

Summer

After hastily visiting the other wards to say hello to the patients, I sat in my car outside the hospital. A light rain drizzled down my windscreen. I was leaving ninety minutes earlier than usual but hoped no one would notice. I pondered the situation with Lucy for what felt like the billionth time. Patients had escaped from the facility on plenty of occasions. They spent months, or even years, building up the trust of the staff to get unsupervised leave. Then the temptation became too much, and they went AWOL. I'd seen it happen at many hospitals, sometimes with devastating consequences. Patients with personality disorders commonly lacked insight into their condition and actions. Empathy was often missing. Any human being who lacked empathy was dangerous in my book. Although I knew of a few people devoid of empathy who were not locked up in a secure hospital.

Runaways sometimes happened even with escorted leave. The patient was not handcuffed to the support worker and the hospital always advised staff not to put their own safety at risk to stop someone from running off. So, although most patients didn't realise it, they could actually run away at any time during leave if they were so inclined. However, with the patient being so ill, they were often not in any fit state of mind to remain hidden. They were far more likely to get drunk, take drugs or cause trouble somewhere, so the police soon found them and brought them back. Actions such as this were partly why it took so long to earn unescorted leave. It was a tremendous security risk and one which always needed to be investigated fully.

What I had never come across was a hospital lying about a missing patient. There simply wasn't any need. Yes, an investigation would be required but, unless it was a regular occurrence, or there were clear signs suggesting leave should not have been granted in the first place, there wasn't any genuine risk to the hospital. A good hospital would not get shut down over one patient escaping, or even two or three. It happened. It was understood that mental illness is an ongoing battle that is difficult or even impossible to *cure*. It wasn't like physical health where it was easy to run a few tests to get confirmation of a disease. A disease which you could cure with drugs and then confirm it had worked by repeating the same tests. You couldn't do a blood test or brain scan and hear the doctor say *yes, you have bi-polar*, or do a brain scan and hear the words *all clear*.

As a responsible clinician, you couldn't use a lie detector test to check if someone is telling you the truth when they promise they're feeling better and won't run away if you give them leave. But there would likely be dismissals, hospital closures, and even possible prison if a patient escaped and the clinician covered it up. That would be a major issue and one which would not go away following a quiet investigation. The risk wasn't worth the severity of the consequences.

I kicked the car into gear and began the drive home. I tried to figure out what *was* worth the risk. What had happened that was so terrible that Dr Rears and even Aaron would cover it up? *Did she sneak out somehow? Was she dead? Had someone murdered her?*

I arrived home twenty minutes later to an empty flat, and slumped onto the sofa, not bothering to remove my shoes or jacket. My mum had picked up Joshua from school and was giving him dinner for me. I'd promised Joshua I would visit him at 6 PM. That gave me two hours. I opened up my phone to look at the names listed in the picture I took of Lucy's file. I didn't know a lot of the staff by name and didn't recognise many. There were lots of staff who couldn't handle it and quickly left, and lots were bank staff rather than permanent fixtures. However, there were two names that caught my eye. One was Dr Rears. He was noted as Lucy's psychiatrist and RC. A strange mixture of relief and anger ran through me. I knew he had been lying to me. The question I needed to answer was *why*. Why would he risk his prominent career over one escaped patient when he was so close to retirement? I knew the answer to that part. He wouldn't risk his career or notoriety for *any* patient. He was selfish and egotistical. *So why risk it all over Lucy?*

The other name I recognised on the list was Aaron. It listed him as Lucy's lead nurse. Another liar. Another narcissist? I struggled to believe it. Aaron had always seemed so genuine in the days of getting drunk together as students. Back then, he appeared to be honest, caring, easygoing. I had never seen him show a nasty bone in his body. That didn't mean he didn't have one, of course. But it was unthinkable to me that he was somehow in league with Dr Rears, especially after I had shared my body with him. Something was making him lie though. Or someone.

I looked again at the list, moving my eyes down past staff names, and noticed a section underneath labeled *family contacts*. I expected that section to be empty. However, there was one name, Hannah Bridgeford. According to this document, Hannah was Lucy's sister. The part of her file I had managed to read earlier did not mention a sister or any other siblings. It may be a foster sister, I supposed. They did have different surnames. Both Hannah's phone number and address were listed. 12 Coppice Court, Edwinstowe. About an hour away from my own home. I felt my excitement growing. I was getting close to the truth. This sister could be the answer to my problems.

I wondered if Hannah still spoke to Lucy, or were they like Eddie and me? So close when we were young, but oceans apart since psychosis took him over. I thought about Eddie often, probably once a day. Sometimes I envisioned our reunion. He would tell me how sorry he was for the attack and that he'd forgiven me for calling the police. He would tell me he is all better now, so there was no need to worry about him being around Joshua. Dylan and Mum would be with us. One big, happy family.

A bang at my door shook me out of my fantasy. What the hell was that? It sounded like one big knock. My heart thumped as I tentatively walked out of the living room to look at the front door.

"Hello?" I called out loudly and instantly regretted it. Now they would know I was inside. As I stood in my hallway frozen with fear, nothing happened. There was no answer, no banging, no footsteps. Was I hearing things now as well? *I am not crazy. I am not seeing things. I am not hearing things.*

I turned my attention back to the phone in my hand. Hannah Bridgeford. What would she think of Lucy's disappearance? She must at least admit Lucy existed and confirm I wasn't having hallucinations. I punched in Hannah's number before I had a chance to think about what to say. I was still scrutinising the front door, as if it was going to explode at any minute. I racked my brain as I waited for the phone to connect, maybe I should say I'm calling to speak about Lucy to see what Hannah's reaction was. But to my dismay, a dial tone greeted me, and a female voice told me that the phone number was no longer in use. There was one other thing I could think to do. I needed to pay Hannah Bridgeford a visit.

22

Summer

Later that evening, I was back at my mum's house. Joshua was happy to sleep at hers again as long as I tucked him in. I stayed with him this time. The bang on the door to my flat had made me even more nervous. We shared the double bed in the spare room, though I pushed the bed right up to the wall. That meant no one could get to Joshua without getting past me. He was out of reach. I slept far better, knowing he was safe next to me.

The next morning I had no visits booked until 2 PM. I was due at another hospital called Antwelle Health Services in Radcliffe-On-Trent for two ward visits, one female and one male personality disorder ward.

Usually, I would have used the lack of morning visits to complete mundane admin tasks, such as writing up my notes and sending them to Natalie for review. I briefly wondered what she would think if she knew I planned on visiting Hannah Bridgeford. It was likely that I'd be formally disciplined, if not sacked. I needed to play it safe. I could not lose my job. The last thing I wanted was to end up as a single mother on benefits. I'd been there when Richard first walked out on me. I wondered again if I should contact Natalie about Lucy, but discarded the idea. She wouldn't help me the last time a patient was in trouble, so I saw no point in telling her now. I pushed her out of my mind.

I jumped into the car to drive home, shower, and change whilst Mum took Joshua to school. I even put some makeup on, a little foundation, blusher, and mascara, with a smattering of lipstick. It was a small amount, but it made me feel confident. Like I used to feel as a young student ready to take on the world, rather than the meeker version of myself I appeared to have become. I didn't like looking in the mirror these days, all I saw were eye bags and tired skin, but a bit of makeup helped. Once I felt more confident, I began the drive to Edwinstowe, merging on to the M1. It was fresh outside, and the cold air pinched my face. It was getting closer to winter weather as November fast approached. I hated being cold. I was much happier feeling warm rays of sunshine on my skin. But I loved this time of year. I loved Halloween and bonfire night. I adored Christmas and New Year. The family time with Joshua and Dylan, the food, the presents, and the fireworks. But mainly, it was the joy. I loved seeing Joshua so happy.

As I trundled along in the left lane, I gave Kelly a quick call. I felt I needed to tell someone what I was doing, just in case. In case of what, I was unsure, but I knew I would feel happier if someone else was aware of where I was going. Kelly didn't answer, though, so I used the in-car system to send her a voice text.

"Hey, Kelly, I'm on the way to Edwinstowe. What you up to? I'll tell you about Edwinstowe later, but I'm visiting a house on Coppice Court. Speak later."

I hoped my text didn't worry her too much. I tried to keep it casual, but the message did still sound strange. Plus, she seemed to have an instinctive knowledge of whenever something was upsetting me.

I approached an old car doing well below the speed limit in the left lane of the motorway, so put on my indicator and moved over to the second lane to overtake, as did the FIAT Punto behind me. When I returned to the left lane, so too did the vehicle behind me. This in itself didn't deter me, but there was something about the car I disliked. I felt as if I'd seen it before. It gave me an uneasy feeling, and I slowed down to see if the car overtook me as well. As I carefully reduced my speed, the car swerved out into the second lane and overtook me. Thank God. I really was paranoid.

I arrived in Edwinstowe an hour later, as the sat nav had informed me I would. I turned on to Coppice Court and drove slower to read the numbers. It wasn't a long street. All the houses mirrored each other in their style of build. All were semi-detached with one-car driveways. I disliked streets where all the houses matched. I much prefer a mismatched street, full of character and intrigue.

Coppice Court was a tired-looking street. I assumed the houses were from the sixties with their style of build. They were all built from a dirty shade of red brick with ancient roofs barely clinging on.

I approached number 12 about halfway down the street. It was a property that had not seen much love recently. Tall weeds rose through the cracks in the paving. The UPVC front door was supposed to be white, but dirt made it appear much darker, and it was unevenly hinged. Grey nets in the dirty windows blocked the view to the inside of the house. It was not an inviting home. Everything about it screamed at me to leave it well alone.

I drove to the end of the street and around the corner, parking well away from number twelve. I walked back to the house with my large parka hood pulled right over my head, trying to ignore the light drizzle that had started. I dawdled as I attempted to make a plan. I did not want to tell Hannah who I actually was as I didn't want to get sacked. At first, I wanted to watch the property to see who lived there. I wanted to check Hannah out before I started asking her questions. I stood across the street, half-hidden behind a tree, pretending to be typing on my phone so I would look less conspicuous.

There were few cars on the road, so I assumed most of Hannah's neighbours were at work. Though when I glanced up at number 12, I froze in fear. The car from the motorway was now parked directly outside of number twelve. There was an enormous figure in the passenger's seat. A man, although I couldn't see his face well. A smaller figure was in the driver's seat, wearing a dark hoodie. I couldn't see them clearly, but they could see me. They were staring right at me.

I pulled my hood further up in a futile attempt to hide and turned around to rush back to the car. Alarm bells rang in every part of my body. Wishing I hadn't parked so far away, I began to run back to the car. I was so close to the end of the road when I heard an engine revving up. I looked behind me. The car was moving straight towards me.

Terror grabbed me, but for once, I didn't freeze from fear. I realised I wasn't going to make it to the car so scanned the street, searching for somewhere to hide. The pavement was wide and open, they could easily drive onto it to hit me. I ducked down behind a large van and hurried to a nearby garden. I hid right behind the car parked in the stranger's driveway, praying the owner of the property would not come out and give me away.

I couldn't see anything from my hiding position, but I did hear the car screech to a stop and its door open and slam shut. The thud of slow footsteps on the pavement made my heartbeat quicken as I thought about Joshua. I was stupid to have come here and put myself in danger when I needed to be around for him. I felt tears coming and desperately pushed them back.

It felt like hours had passed, but it was probably seconds before the car door opened and shut again. I heard the car drive away, but stayed glued to the spot. I couldn't move. What if they were tricking me and one of them was still out there? I willed myself to breathe again, staying as quiet as possible. My legs were rooted to the spot, and blood pounded in my ears, making it difficult to hear anything. As the street stayed silent, I realised I had to risk looking out past the car I was hiding behind if I wanted to get away.

Daylight seared my eyes as I slowly cracked them open. I blinked, trying to get used to the light, and turned to my left to snake my head around the car. Two green eyes stared straight back at me.

23

Summer

My vision had blurred from clamping my eyes shut so hard. Lucy's eyes glared brightly and, for a moment, they were all I could see. As my vision adjusted, I noticed the plump features of her face, her wrinkled, soft skin, and a normal nose that did not resemble a burnt stump. Her fine, grey hair was curled from a perm. The green eyes were worried and warm rather than cold. It dawned on me that this was not Lucy. It was likely the lady who lived in the house behind me. I attempted to apologise, but all that escaped my lips was a stutter.

"Are you okay, dear?" The lady's voice was soft, full of concern. It had a slight whine to it, like elderly people's often did.

"Yes, yes, I'm so sorry. I was…er…I'll go now." I forced myself to stand, but winced as I did so. Pain jumped up both legs like tiny bee stings after being bent uncomfortably for so long.

"No." Her face was lined with worry. "No, no. Don't run off. Come and have a cup of tea."

She put a withered hand on my arm to guide me. I smiled gratefully and allowed her to lead me inside the house. It looked like number 12 from the outside, but the door was a dark purple. The windowsills were still white and much cleaner than number 12. There were no weeds in the driveway, and a neat patch of grass lay to the left, surrounded by colourful flowers. I followed the lady through the front door and into a narrow corridor. I couldn't help but smile at the décor. The carpet was a deep red with a repeating pattern of huge purple flowers. The walls were a faded cream, and photos lined the corridor. There were many different shapes and sizes of photos, and mainly of one particular boy. He actually looked vaguely familiar to me, though I was in no state to figure out why. We entered an open doorway before the stairs and walked into a lounge. The carpet was the same, but the walls were a dull peach colour. They were lined with more photos of the same boy and different styles of clocks. None of the furniture in the room matched.

"Now, you take a seat here while I get you some sweet tea," she said sternly, pushing me towards the sofa.

"Water is fine." I managed. My stomach churned at the thought of forcing down sweet tea. I smiled at her to show I was not being rude.

"Okay, water it is then." She smiled back at me and gestured again for me to sit. I obeyed and perched on the sofa. My breathing was beginning to slow again, although I still felt a little weak. The walls of the old lady's house were a barricade between me and whoever the hell had chased me. Surely that wasn't Lucy. How would she have gotten a car, and what reason would she have to drive it at me? I cursed myself for not getting the registration number. The old lady returned within a couple of minutes with my glass of water, which I accepted gratefully.

"Is there someone I can call for you?" She looked at me warily as she spoke, like she was trying to figure out if I was going to panic again.

"Er, no…I'm fine now, honestly. My car is around the corner. I'll go back to it in a sec and get out of your way," I replied. I hoped I sounded better than I felt.

"What happened? Has someone hurt you?" she asked.

"Oh, no!" I smiled again. "It was nothing…really..I..er…had a panic attack. I suffer from anxiety. I needed a space to calm down again but didn't quite make it to my car."

The old lady gave me an understanding nod. "Do you have far to drive home?"

"Oh no, to the other side of town. I was here to see an old friend, but she doesn't appear to be at home." The lady seemed sweet, but I lied all the same.

"Oh?" The lady posed this as a question. "Who is your friend? I know most of the street. Lived here for 56 years now!"

I examined the elderly woman for a moment. "Hannah," I answered.

"Hannah?" Her forehead wrinkled.

"Yes. Hannah Bainbridge. I think she lives at number 12?"

"Number 12? Oh, dear honey, I think you must have the wrong street. There's no Hannah at number 12." She looked at me again with concern in her eyes.

"Do you know who lives there?" I ventured tentatively. I wasn't sure if I wanted to know.

"Why yes, an older man, although I forget his name. He's a doctor, I think."

For a moment, it didn't register. But slowly, it dawned on

me who the large man in that car must have been.

"Dr Rears?" My voice was a whisper.

"Yes! That's it! Rears. Is Hannah a relative of his? I do see some young women visiting from time to time."

"You do? What do they look like?" The words rushed out, and the lady looked at me in surprise.

"Well...they are a bit strange." She started slowly, seeming to struggle for an appropriate description. "I can't see that far these days, but there is one lady who visits on a Sunday. She is quite petite with black hair and doesn't dress too good, if I'm honest. I keep my distance. I'm not one to judge people, but sometimes you know, don't you?" She looked at me for approval for her judgmental attitude.

"Know what?" I prompted again.

She looked hard at me for a moment before deciding to trust me with her opinions. "She isn't all there," she whispered, as though someone else might hear. Raising her voice back to normal levels, she added, "I think she must have had a terrible accident a few weeks ago. Strange marks all over her face." She looked at me sadly.

"Marks?" I prompted her.

"Yes. It looked like scarring from this far away. Like maybe she had been burnt. Awful stuff."

My stomach did a somersault. Lucy must have been at number 12 with Dr Rears, but her face had been burnt a long time ago. So the previous lady could not have been Lucy.

"What did she look like before the burns?" I asked.

"Well, she had lighter hair then. More brown than black. Still dressed the same, in old clothes every week she was." She tutted as if not dressing well was a crime to be ashamed of. "Could have been such a pretty girl if she had taken better care of herself. Now I suppose her accident means she will care even less."

I had no idea who the other woman might be, but it was clear that the lady was talking about two different women, even if she didn't realise it herself. The previous one had no scars on her face, and the one more recently with a scarred face. And Dr Rears had brought them to his home. A stormy wave of fury flowed through me at the thought. There was so much more to this than Lucy. I needed to get home. I needed to speak to someone. Someone I should have spoken to when all of this first started.

24

Summer

Two hours later, I was home alone. I had called in sick to Antwelle Health Services. Unless I had a stomach bug, I rarely called into work sick. Hospital rules stated we could not return until we had been well for a minimum of forty-eight hours following a sick bug, as the last thing they needed was it flying through all the patients and staff. So this was the excuse I used. It gave me a minimum of three days off work and was never questioned. I had slight paranoia that the law of karma meant I would end up actually being ill soon, but I pushed the concern away. Sometimes you have to tell lies to get to the truth.

Joshua was still at school. Mum was going to pick him up. She normally did when I was at work, anyway. I should be more grateful, and maybe take her out for dinner once this was over. Though the thought that she might decline put me off. Until I knew what had happened and Lucy was back at the hospital, I wanted Joshua to remain safely away from the house. I couldn't be sure if it was her that had nearly run me over, but it certainly looked like her. The car had disappeared when I left the old lady's house, who I'd found out was named Mrs Timpson.

I now sat back at my kitchen table with my phone, ready to make the call. I groaned inwardly at the thought, but I knew I had to do it. I had to call Natalie.

"Hey, Summer," Natalie answered after the first ring, eager as ever.

"Hey," I said, less enthusiastically. "You got a sec to talk?"

"Sure."

"Great. It's...it's a bit strange." I wasn't sure how to tell her, so I jumped right in. "There's a patient at Derby Hospital by the name of Lucy Clarke. Yet, she isn't there anymore. And when I asked her nurse and psychiatrist where she was, they said they'd never heard of her."

"What?" Natalie's voice was full of confusion. She was quiet for a moment. "Maybe she's from a different hospital?"

I rolled my eyes. Of course she fucking wasn't. "No, she was definitely in Derby. It's a bit weird, isn't it? I don't get why they'd lie?"

"I doubt they're lying, Summer." She scoffed. I put my head in my hands to keep the bubbling anger in check. I knew she'd be no help.

"Well, I've found her patient file on their computer. They have changed it to a different name." I delivered my evidence, expecting this to make her see that they *were* lying.

"Oh. Well, ask some other staff. I'm sure someone knows where she went. Probably a transfer."

I couldn't tell Natalie about my visit to Edwinstowe, so I wasn't sure how to get her to see the seriousness of what was happening.

"Yes, I will," I said instead. "But to be honest, Natalie, I think something strange is going on."

"Okay. Well, let me speak to Alexia, see if she has any ideas."

I rolled my eyes for the third time before letting her know about my sick bug and saying goodbye. I didn't know what I'd expected her to say, but I'd hoped for some agreement that it was a strange situation at least. I prepared my phone for the next call, another one I didn't want to make.

"Hello, Derby Police," a female voice answered.

"Hi, my name is Summer Thomas. I need to speak to somebody about a missing patient."

"Hello again, Ms Thomas."

"Er, again? No, I haven't called you before," I said with a voice full of indignation. *What was she talking about?*

"Okay, Ms Thomas, I'll see if I can put you through to DI Swanson again," she sighed loudly.

Music blared in my ear before I could respond. I lowered the phone and checked at the screen. I'd dialed the right number, but I had never called it before in my life. Less than a minute later, a deep male voice came on the line.

"DI Swanson," he said.

"Er, yes, hi, my name is Summer Thomas."

"Yes, Ms Thomas, I remember," he replied in a snappy tone.

"No, you don't." I snapped back. "We've never spoken." I heard him mutter something under his breath.

"Did you curse?" I asked him.

"Let me guess, a patient named Lucy Clarke is missing, and no one will admit it," he replied, still in the same curt tone. It stunned me into silence. I had no idea how to respond. "Well?" he insisted.

"Wh…I…yes," I said, stumbling over my words.

"Hmm, well, how did I know that if we've never spoken

before?"

"I...I don't know. How did you know? Are you trying to tell me I told you this? When?" I demanded.

"Every day since Friday, Ms Thomas."

"I have never called you!"

"Well, you do sound different. Kudos for putting on a voice, but we both know the truth, don't we?"

"I'm telling you, I have never spoken to you!" I said, my voice getting louder.

"Look, Ms Thomas, I've told you before that I will look into Lucy Clarke's whereabouts. If you don't remember, then please contact your doctor." And with those words, Swanson hung up the phone and left me sitting open-mouthed at my kitchen table.

I thought about the likelihood that someone had been calling the police since Friday pretending to be me. Statistically, I knew it was more likely I was losing my mind, but I refused to believe it. Someone was messing with me. Aaron's voice was too deep to pretend to be me, the same for Dr Rears, that left Lucy herself.

I didn't know what to do next. If I called Kelly, would she think I was crazy too and tell me to see a doctor? What would Natalie think? She was no use at the best of times. Or my mum, who was already terrified that Dylan or I might get ill like Eddie? There was no one I could turn to.

Hot tears ran down my cheeks, and I was drawn back to my phone. Aaron had called me three times, but I hadn't answered any of them. I wanted to speak to him to tell him I had found Lucy's file photo and had proof of her existence. Now a surge of loneliness was ripping through me and I ached to be with him, even if he was lying. I was stuck in a nightmare, and no one could wake me up.

One person who always made me feel better, though, was Joshua. I forced myself to stand on wobbly legs and walked to the sink to splash my face. I needed to think straight. I considered what to say or ask Aaron when I called him. I wanted to prepare for either more lies or the truth. I had a feeling that the truth was not going to be happy news, but it was vital for me to be able to defend Joshua. My phone buzzed to indicate I had received a text message. I unlocked it to take a look.

Aaron: *Please pick up. Just want to make sure you're okay. xx*

I found that strange. Why wouldn't I be okay if Lucy was dead, as he claimed? I replied to tell him I was fine, but busy, and would call him soon. Despite our last argument, he was still my closest link to the truth. He replied again.

Aaron: *Ring me now please–it's urgent xxx*

I rolled my eyes. I didn't have the energy to deal with him lying yet again. But then it might be something to do with Lucy. I selected the call button next to his text message and held the phone to my ear. It barely rang before I heard his voice.

"Summer? Hey." He fell silent, seemingly unsure what to say now that he had my attention.

"Hey." There was still silence from his end. "What's so urgent?"

"Err," he paused, "can you meet me somewhere? Somewhere quiet, where we won't be followed. Just in case...ya know... my ex..." He added hastily. "The car park at the supermarket? The underground part."

"I don't know, Aaron. I'm exhausted." I yawned loudly, evidencing my point.

"Please. It's about Lucy."

He'd piqued my interest. Should I tell him about Dr Rears? I decided not to, wanting to see what he had to say first.

"Why can't you tell me over the phone?" I asked. I didn't want to go out again, despite wanting to be close to him a few minutes earlier.

"Please, come see me now. Trust me?"

He had a nerve asking for trust after lying to me, but I caved and agreed to meet him. My loneliness was too much. I was unsettled by the whole thing, though I couldn't put my finger on exactly what was bothering me. I still did not believe Aaron was a danger to me. Still, as a precaution I called Kelly. The phone rang and rang. I was about to hang up when she finally answered. I explained everything that had happened in the last forty-eight hours as briefly as I could. Though, I didn't tell her about the car trying to run me off the pavement, or about the police saying I'd called them. I didn't want her to panic.

"I'm going to meet Aaron at the supermarket car park," I said.

"I'm coming with you. Give me twenty mins to pull a sickie from work. I'll meet you there."

I agreed, but I didn't want to drag Kelly into it any deeper, so I set off straight away instead. Now that someone knew where I was going, I was a bit more at ease. I could meet Aaron and then talk it over with Kelly when she arrived. I'd tell her in full then. It was Aaron after all, and Aaron would not hurt me.

25

Summer

Ten minutes later, I drove into the underground car park, watching for any sign of Lucy whilst also looking out for Aaron. The supermarket had arranged the car park as one giant level underground, rather than having many floors. It was dank, and the thick smell of oil burnt my nostrils. There was a vast outdoor car park, so the underground one seldom got used. There were less than a dozen cars parked in spaces far away from each other, most of them likely belonging to the staff. It took my eyes a minute to adjust, and the weak wall lights didn't help that much. It was another long minute before I saw Aaron lurking in the far right corner.

I considered driving off for a moment as a pang of fear clutched me, but I knew that was silly. It was Aaron, for god's sake. I had known him for years. I knew he was a good guy. Whatever reason he had for not confiding in me, he wouldn't hurt me. I eased my car closer to Aaron. I hated underground car parks. The spaces were always far too narrow. All my previous cars had been worth less than a grand, and I'd bumped every one of them in similar car parks, or at least whilst parking. So I was wary of scratching the BMW and chose a spot about five spaces away from Aaron.

As I turned off the ignition, I realised how much I did not want to be there. It didn't feel safe. I was tempted to drive away from the situation then and there. But thoughts of getting to the truth to ensure Joshua's safety made me stay. I contemplated waiting for Kelly, but didn't want to drag her into a potentially dangerous situation, either. I sighed. I knew I had to speak to Aaron alone. Slowly, I opened the door and looked up at Aaron. I wasn't in a rush to see him. My earlier loneliness had vanished, and I suddenly craved being alone.

"Hey." He smiled at me meekly. He seemed wary too. He moved from one foot to the other, and his eyes darted around the car park. His usual easy manner was nowhere to be seen.

"Hey, weirdo." I tried to break the awkwardness with a smile. "What have you called me here for then?" My tone was light-hearted. Or at least that's what I aimed for.

He smiled back weakly for a second. "There's something else I need to tell you about Lucy."

"Yes, you said on the phone." I dropped my smile. I couldn't be bothered to pretend anymore. "But I want no more lies, Aaron."

"No. No more lies. Pinkie promise." He stuck out his little finger.

I rolled my eyes. "So you admit you lied to me about Lucy, then? You know she isn't a ghost."

"I didn't lie. Have you seen the plaque?"

I nodded my head in response.

"So you know there was a Lucie Clarke who died in the fire?" Aaron asked.

"Yes. A different Lucy, clearly. Their names aren't even spelt the same."

"Yes. A different Lucy," he admitted, finally.

"So… Why lie to me?"

"I didn't want to lie, Summer. I was trying to protect you."

"From who? From Lucy?"

"No, not Lucy!"

"Then who, Aaron? Who were you trying to protect me from?"

"I need to ask you something first. Why are you so bothered?" Aaron surveyed me with serious eyes.

"What kind of question is that?" I was getting more and more frustrated with his strange behaviour. " "Tell me what happened to Lucy!"

"Not until you answer my question. Why do you care what happened to her? Didn't you fall out with her and tell everyone not to allow her into the ward round?"

"She's my patient! Of course, I care about what happens to her. I'm her advocate. I'm here to speak for her when she can't speak for herself. And no, I didn't tell them anything. I would never suggest not doing a ward round for a patient. It's their right, and they're entitled to one, in my opinion!"

When I finished, Aaron was silent, as if trying to figure me out. I wondered if he actually had the balls to accuse me of being the dishonest one after all of his lies to me.

"To be honest, you're freaking me out, Aaron. Tell me the truth now, or I'm leaving."

"I know Lucy," he blurted out. I stared at him, willing him to continue. "I know Lucy," he repeated, slower and calmer. "And I know what happened to her."

"Yes, Aaron, I've figured that bit out. Now please tell me."

"What will you do when you know?" he asked.

"How do I know? I don't know what happened yet!" My voice was raised and bristled with frustration.

"Will you go to the authorities?" he asked.

"Well, yes, if I need to!" Days of confusion and fear were getting to me at this point. I was fast losing the grip on my usual cool exterior. And because it was Aaron I was talking to, I forgot to say the right things as I would when trying to get a patient to open up to me.

I was off my guard and didn't hear the footsteps creeping up behind me. By the time I noticed the shadow on my right side, it was too late. I saw a flash of green eyes before everything went black.

26

Swanson

DI Alex Swanson sat in his cramped and jumbled office outside the City Centre. The paperwork crowding the office belied the fact that Swanson was usually exceptionally organised when it came to his work in the Special Operations Unit: Major Crime. At that moment, however, he sat contemplating his phone and trying to figure out what the hell had taken place about twenty minutes before.

It was the fourth call this week from Summer Thomas. She sounded different. Her voice was much smoother, but that wasn't what was bothering him. Anyone could change their voice. There was an odd note to her voice that hadn't been there before. That note had settled uncomfortably in his mind, like a seed that he was not willing to grow. Swanson was far too busy to be looking for ghostly patients, but he couldn't throw the thought that maybe someone was fucking with both him and this Summer Thomas. He couldn't tell if she was lying over the phone. He considered meeting up with her, but what would they gain? More confusion and lies? He wasn't sure there was any point.

He had already had a discussion with Derby Hospital the previous day, and had spoken to the lead psychiatrist from the ward, Dr Rears. The doctor had confirmed there was not a Lucy Clark on Bluebell Ward or their other female ward. Although, there had been a Lucie Clarke who died in a fire a few years before. Dr Rears had also told him about the patients getting worked up over ghosts sometimes. It had seriously creeped Swanson out. Murderers, kidnappers, thieves he could deal with. They were an actual threat. You could see them, talk to them, hurt them, and best of all, catch them. But scary burnt ghosts who you couldn't touch or see? *Fuck that.* Swanson didn't even watch ghost films.

The last thing he wanted to do was visit that creepy hospital again. He had visited the hospital a few times. Violence, theft accusations, and absconded patients all brought him there a couple of times a year. It was a hub of constant crime, and full to the rafters of murderers, paedophiles, rapists and stalkers. Maybe googling Summer's employer would help, they might have a picture of her or a staff profile. He cursed as he realised he didn't know the name, and he had to use the hospital website to find out which advocacy company they used. Once he'd found it, he located the company website—Rowan's Advocacy. It looked appropriate enough, with lots of information on mental health. He noticed a page titled *Meet our Advocates* and clicked upon it. He scrolled down through the list. It started with a serious-looking older woman named Alexia. The boss by the sound of it. He kept scrolling and flicking through the other people. *David Geraghty. Natalie Brown.* Eventually, near the bottom, he found *Summer Thomas.* His eyes were drawn to her picture first. Light brown hair fell loose around her breasts. Her blue eyes were shy, as was her smile. She looked sweet, calm, and younger than he had thought she was, maybe in her mid to late twenties. He read her profile.

Summer Thomas holds a first class honours degree in Psychology from Derby University, where she also won Volunteer of The Year, Student Union Person of The Year, and published her undergraduate research to worldwide acclaim. Summer went on to achieve a Masters in Forensic Psychology from the University of Nottingham, where she completed her research and also won yet another award for creating and delivering innovative life skills classes for adults with autism. Summer covers the East Midlands area and dedicates herself to helping adults with mental health issues and learning disabilities.

Jesus fucking Christ. Looks, brains, and spending her life helping others. Why would this seemingly perfect overachiever be calling him constantly about a missing patient who didn't exist? Then again, the good ones always turned out to be nuts. He sat back at his desk and checked the time. It was five past three. The door to his office opened noisily, causing his neck to snap up from his laptop. His usual partner, DI Rebecca Hart, stood in the doorway.

"What are you doing?" she asked him sharply. Her head was tilted to one side, and her short, dark hair bobbed around her chin.

"Remember that nutcase Summer Thomas who keeps refusing to speak to anyone but me?" he asked.

She rolled her eyes and nodded.

"Well, she called again. She sounded different, though. So I checked her out. Come look at this."

Hart strode towards his desk. She never walked. One would think she was meek because of her small and skinny frame, especially when she stood next to Swanson, but she was the opposite. Loud, purposeful, and striding everywhere she went. She bent over his desk to look at the screen. Her strong, flowery perfume stung his nostrils. She spent a minute reading the text about Summer. Her small nose wrinkled with disgust.

"She sounds awful, doesn't she?" She didn't look at him as she spoke.

"Awful?" Swanson looked at her with raised eyebrows.

"Full of herself. All those awards and qualifications. Who cares?" She shrugged her shoulders and walked back towards the office door. "I'm going for lunch. I forgot to eat earlier. Want to come?"

"Okay." Swanson wasn't hungry, but he wanted to convince her that there was something off about the calls from Summer Thomas. He stood and grabbed his coat to leave with her. As he started to walk away, the shrill noise of his desk phone rang out.

"Leave it." Hart rolled her eyes again. "Come on. I'm hungry."

He ignored her and answered his phone.

"Hi…Er…DI Swanson." It was the same receptionist from earlier. "I've heard about something I thought you'd be interested in. It's about Summer Thomas."

His interest piqued, he turned his back to Hart so he could ignore her mouthing at him to hurry up.

"Go on," he said, pen poised above his desk notepad.

"Well, her friend has reported her missing."

"Missing? She called me less than an hour ago."

"Yes..she's missing under suspicious circumstances."

27

Summer

A sharp pain shot through the back of my head as I tried to open my eyes. I managed a split second before they involuntarily closed. A mass of dark shapes attacked my vision each time I opened them. It wasn't until I tried to raise my hands to rub my throbbing eyes that I realised I couldn't move. Something prevented my hands from moving any further than the small of my back. Fear stifled my throat, and a damp smell filled my nostrils. It felt like water surrounded me, yet despite the darkness, I knew I was surrounded by air. Thoughts of Joshua filled my head, causing panic to pull at my stomach. *How could I be stupid enough to let myself end up in this position? What would happen to him if I died cold and alone?*

In order to get back to him I needed to stay calm. I stopped trying to raise my arms and lay still instead. I listened. The silence pummelled my eardrums more than any noise I could ever remember. I used my body to test out my surroundings whilst my eyes adjusted to the dark. I was lying on my side. My face was against something cold and hard. I thought it was concrete at first, but it was too rough against my hands and face. It felt more like a stone floor.

I tried to piece together what had happened and figure out where I was. I reached out to the last fuzzy image in my mind of Aaron's face. He was talking about Lucy. I knew he hadn't told me where she was. We hadn't gotten that far. I had heard a noise and turned around. I remembered a flash of green eyes, pain in my head. And then I had awoken in the dark hell hole, unable to move my hands. Panic grabbed at my chest again. I closed my eyes and told myself sternly I would not die. I was going to get Joshua, find a new home, and forget all about this fucking mess. First things first, though. I had to figure out where I was and who had hit me. I knew it wasn't Aaron. He had been a few feet in front of me. The flash of green I had seen may have been Lucy, but I couldn't be sure.

There was no way Aaron had stood there as Lucy attacked me. It didn't make sense, so I concentrated instead on my surroundings. I could figure out the who later. My eyes were beginning to adjust to the gloom, and the edges of some shapes were becoming less blurry. I blinked again and finally noticed the thin shadow standing before me. I shrank back as much as I could in my awkward position on the floor. As my eyes adjusted further, I realised it was a person with slicked-back hair. They were wearing dark trousers and some sort of hoodie. I couldn't make out the face, but the eyes gave her away.

Lucy bent down and leaned towards me, her eyes glaring into my own. Her face was so close to mine that I could feel her stale breath. Her stench filled my nostrils. It was so bad I thought I would never be able to smell anything else for the rest of my life. That was probably true, as my life was possibly about to be cut short.

Her scarred face was clear by then, even in the dark. I wriggled back again as she leaned closer, trying to move my hands or stand or at least sit, but my feet were also tied. I was trapped. It made no sense that skinny Lucy could have tied me this tightly. That's when I remembered Aaron. I looked around the room, searching for Aaron. I didn't know if he was in on this attack or if he was hurt, too. He was my one chance, and I prayed he was nearby and would help me. I spotted Aaron sitting on the floor about twenty feet behind Lucy. He'd brought his knees up to his face, and his arms were resting on them, one elbow on each knee. He didn't look tied up. His head was bent towards the ground, and I couldn't see if his eyes were opened or closed.

"Aaron?" My voice sounded strange, like it was faraway. There was a slight echo reminiscent of being in a cave. Aaron didn't move.

"Summer!" Lucy exclaimed in an excited tone. Her face moved closer, her nose almost touching mine. She had blocked my view of Aaron. "It's me. Lucy?" She cocked her head to one side like a confused puppy.

I looked back at her, not sure what to say.

"Hi, Lucy," I ventured. It was all I could manage to force out of my dry throat.

"Hi!" she replied, as though we were long-lost friends. "I'm so glad you're finally here, Summer. I need you. Thanks for coming!" She nodded her head enthusiastically. Lucy was a different woman than when I had last seen her on the ward. She was my friend again.

"It's okay, Summer," Aaron mumbled from behind Lucy. Lucy shifted to look at him, and Aaron came back into my view. He had looked up, but he was rubbing his head as though it ached. "Lucy, untie Summer now."

"You need me?" I said blankly to Lucy. Confusion distorted my thoughts, and I couldn't decide who to focus on. Lucy turned back towards me as Aaron attempted to stand.

"Well, yes. You are still my advocate, aren't you? Your job is to speak for me?"

I didn't know what to say to her. "Well, I was, but then you went missing."

She laughed, the high-pitched, girly sound echoing in the strange room. "Yes, I ran off, thanks to *them!*" She spat the last word. Someone had clearly upset her. Multiple people by the sound of it.

"Them?" It seemed I was still incapable of forming a complete sentence.

"Yesss, them!" She pronounced each word slowly as if I were a child or an idiot.

I tried to sit up and Lucy jumped forward. Her cold hands twisted around the tops of my arms, her nails digging deep. I flinched and tried to shift back. To my surprise, she hauled me up and helped me lean against the damp wall behind me. I eyed her suspiciously as she moved back to sit on her knees again. There was now a gap of about three feet between us. Blood rushed to my head, and I closed my eyes and waited for the dizziness to pass. When I opened them again, Lucy was still eyeing me, and Aaron was back on the floor. Apparently, standing hadn't gone too well.

"Why am I tied up, Lucy?" I asked in a gentle voice. I didn't want to make her angry. She was not mad at me yet, and I didn't appear to be included in *them*.

"Oh, ya know, so you don't run off," she said as if it was the most obvious thing in the world.

"I won't run off, Lucy," I replied cautiously, "but my hands are really hurting."

"Okay, soon," she said. She sounded sincere, and hope started to replace my panic.

I threw another look over at Aaron. He was attempting to stand again, but Lucy paid him no attention.

"Is Aaron okay?" I asked Lucy, since she seemed more chatty than usual.

"No, not really," she replied. I waited for her to elaborate, but she didn't. Instead, she stood and walked towards Aaron.

I took the opportunity to force my wrists out of what felt like a zip tie, but it was no use. It was too tight, and pulling made it dig in more. I gave up and tried to bring her attention back to me so Aaron could do what he needed to get us out of here.

"Untie me and tell me what you need," I said, still keeping my voice light and friendly.

She turned back around and looked at me, her eyes suddenly full of suspicion.

"I will tell you first, *then* untie you. I need to make sure I can trust you like Aaron said we could," she explained. I threw Aaron a wide-eyed look, suddenly unsure if he would be my saviour. He didn't look up at me.

I turned back to Lucy and found her studying me. Her eyes were wide with fear. I had no idea why *she* was scared, seeing as I was the one trussed up and at the mercy of a violent person with disordered thoughts. A warm trickle of blood ran down my neck as I dutifully nodded my understanding, despite the searing pain in my head.

"I knew complaining to the hospital wouldn't help. That's

why I've brought you here." She hesitated. "I am sorry about your head. It was the only way." Her eyes pleaded with me.

"Oh, okay." I tried to look thoughtful. "I understand."

She nodded back, pleased with my answer. She paced the room, her steps quick. Aaron had managed to stand by then and kept his eyes on her, one hand still resting against the back of his head.

"Don't be mad at Aaron. I needed him to check we could trust you," Lucy said.

I remembered the strange questions Aaron had asked me. *Why did I want to know what happened to Lucy? Would I tell the authorities?*

"You see, that...that...that," Lucy tried to find words that escaped her, "pathetic excuse of a man, is no doctor! He is an abuser." She said this fast, as though the words were poison on her lips. She stopped pacing and looked right at me, gauging my response.

I wasn't sure what to make of her words at first. Lucy was severely ill, and I knew her well enough to know she did lie a lot. All the time, to be frank. Sometimes she suffered psychotic periods where she wasn't lying, but her hallucinations made her believe certain things were happening. Other times she lied because she thought it was funny to do so. But Dr Rears also disgusted me to my core, and I was never sure why. There was something off about him. An unspoken warning I couldn't put my finger on.

"You see, Aaron knows all about this piece of shit. He's seen him, haven't you, Aaron?" She glanced over at him, but did not wait for a response before continuing. Aaron stood leaning against the opposite wall, still watching her. "He knows all about it."

"You need to untie Summer, Lucy," Aaron said again. He could have overpowered her. He was much taller and stronger, but he knew the best way out of the situation was to talk her down. He must have known I would understand what he was trying to do.

"But I don't know, Lucy," I reminded her. "Tell me. Please, let me help."

Lucy sat down to my left, leaning her back against the wall. She was inches away and staring straight at me. I looked into the green eyes that had haunted me since Friday. They weren't cold. At least not at that moment. They were sorrowful and childlike. I realised how ridiculous I'd been. I felt my fear dissolve. Lucy was a lost soul. Like my brother and most of my patients.

"I will tell you, but then you need to tell everybody else." Her eyes implored me. I could see that she was looking for signs of me lying. She was still trying to figure out if she could trust me.

I got it then. She knew they would believe me. She knew they wouldn't believe her, like I'd doubted her. Even though I despised Dr Rears, even though I'd seen his gaze linger on younger patients, and even though I was supposed to be her advocate, I hadn't instantly believed her. Why would the MDT at the hospital or the police? They wouldn't. I wasn't even sure then that I believed her, but that was not my role as an advocate.

"Yes. Okay, Lucy, I will. Now, untie me and tell me what you need people to know."

28

Swanson

Swanson sat in the claustrophobic briefing room with Hart and four police officers initially assigned to Summer's supposed disappearance. His hand absentmindedly stroked his beard. Summer Thomas had absolutely fucked his week up.

"She's probably faking it," Hart said. "She's a nut job."

"So, how many times did she call today?" asked a skinny officer named PC Townsend.

"I dunno. Loads, probably." Hart looked pointedly at Swanson.

Swanson shrugged. "I don't know if she's mentally ill or not," he said. "Talk me through who reported her missing."

"So there was an emergency call from the woman's mum," Townsend began.

"Summer's mum?" Swanson interrupted.

Townsend threw an annoyed look his way. "Yes, Summer's mum. She rang and said a friend of Summer's had told her Summer had been attacked and taken by someone. She didn't know who. So the mum rang emergency services and reported it."

"But how did this friend know, and why didn't they call the police?" Hart asked.

"She did, ten minutes later. She said she had planned to meet Summer and someone else at the car park. When she got there, Summer's car door was wide open, her handbag was on the passenger seat, and there were drops of blood on the floor next to the driver's door," Townsend said.

"What's the friend's name?" asked Swanson.

"Err...Kelly something. I'll need to check."

"Useful." Hart rolled her eyes.

"So the friend saw that, went to the mum's *house* rather than call, and *then* rang the police?" Swanson muttered to himself. The rest of the officers looked at him.

"There's something weird about all this." Hart liked to state the obvious. "Come on, let's go to the car park then."

"I'm not sure there's any reason for major crime to be involved yet," PC Blake, scoffed.

"Well, we are, so deal with it," Hart said before walking away. She looked at Swanson expectedly until he stood and followed.

They made their way together through winding grey corridors to Swanson's black Audi, parked at the back of the station. Hart quickened her pace to keep up with Swanson's long strides. The supermarket's car park Summer had allegedly been taken from was one both of them knew well. They often grabbed lunch or petrol from there whilst working as it wasn't too far from the station. It would take less than ten minutes to drive there.

"So, what do you think happened then?" Hart asked him once they were in the car.

"Fuck knows." Swanson's tone was grim as he reversed out

of the car park space, an inch away from hitting a bollard in his rush.

"I reckon she's staged the whole thing. Rang her mate to meet her, left blood and everything there so we'd come look. She's been trying to get your attention all week with her bullshit story. It would make more sense than any other explanation."

Swanson said nothing. He knew Hart was right. It was the most logical explanation. But there was something about Summer's tone earlier on the phone that made him wonder if perhaps she was telling the truth. They drove through the midday traffic easily. Derby wasn't a big city and only got truly busy at rush hour, football matches, or during road works. He parked neatly in the outdoor car park, near the entrance to the underground space. Cold air whipped around them as they walked towards the pedestrian entrance, where Summer was supposedly taken. Hart pulled the collar of her coat up higher. Swanson hadn't bothered to wear one. Once underground, the pair inspected their surroundings. Few cars occupied any spaces. Despite dim lights on the walls, the atmosphere was gloomy. There was a blue BMW on the far side of the car park that matched the description they had been given. The pair glanced at each other.

"Why would Summer meet her mate here?" asked Hart, filling the silence again.

Swanson ignored her and instead headed towards the car. He surveyed the car park as he walked. Hart followed behind at a slower pace, taking her time. Swanson reached Summer's vehicle and bent down to look inside. Someone had closed the car door, but he noted the handbag on the front seat as Townsend had described. He didn't touch the door or try its handle. Instead, he knelt on the floor to study some dark spots of liquid, which did look like blood as the friend had described. He wondered why Summer might go to this much trouble to reach him.

"Stop," he instructed Hart. She had reached the vehicle and was about to open the door.

"Why? You don't actually think this is real, do you?"

"I don't know. Just don't fuck anything up."

Hart took out a package from her handbag and waved it at Swanson. Gloves. She threw them on and opened the car door. Voices echoed from the pedestrian entrance and the four officers from the briefing room appeared. Hart carried on and picked up the handbag to open it. She rummaged around in the bag and pulled out a purse.

"Yep, it's Summer Thomas," she announced after searching the purse and finding Summer's ID. She replaced the purse and bag in the vehicle as the officers arrived behind her. "You took your time." She raised a perfectly waxed eyebrow.

"Found anything?" PC Blake asked.

Hart proceeded to inform Blake about the handbag and the closed door as Swanson silently wandered off. He walked into the middle of the car park, his dark eyes surveying every nook and cranny of the surroundings. The place was dreary and smelled musty and damp. No one other than the officers had entered since he and Hart arrived. It wouldn't be too hard to have a fight with someone in here and have it go unnoticed. But how would you get an adult out of here against their will? You would need them to be quiet, knocked out cold perhaps. You'd have to be strong or know where to hit someone to knock them out. He flicked his eyes up to the ceiling. He smiled. Cameras. Now they were getting somewhere.

29

Summer

Lucy looked determined. "Okay, I'll untie you." She bent to reach for something on the floor.

There was a slight glint as the weak lights on the wall caught the item within their rays. Scissors. I noticed the wall lights were the same dim lights as in the underground car park. Lucy came closer and used the scissors to cut the zip ties from my wrists and ankles. I winced as she released each one. It was worse than the pain of them cutting against my skin.

"Sorry, Summer," Aaron mumbled. "It was the only way." He still stood over by the far wall.

He watched Lucy the entire time, never taking his eyes off her. I don't know why he bothered. If she'd been messing with us and actually went to stab me, he would have been much too far away to stop her. I shot him an angry look as I rubbed each wrist and ankle in turn, trying to rub away the pain. How could this possibly have been the only way? I concentrated on Lucy since she still had the scissors in her hand and was close enough to reach out and stab me. I cursed as I realised my phone was sitting on the passenger seat of my car.

"What's wrong? Is that not better?" Lucy smiled sweetly. That was the first time I'd seen her smile so widely. With her scarred face, it wasn't a pretty sight, but she seemed to feel guilty for hurting me.

"Yes, thanks, Lucy." I felt some claustrophobia lift when I could move more freely and my eyes had fully adjusted.

I scanned the room again, and noted there was a heavy metal door behind Aaron which looked like a fire door. I'd need to stand to have a chance at reaching the door, but Lucy was in my way. I had to stay calm and think my way out. She was too unpredictable. To the left of me were stacks of boxes. Dozens and dozens of them with black writing, though I couldn't keep my head turned away for long enough to read them. I wanted to ensure I didn't lose my bond with her. She may have been a lost soul, but she was also mentally ill with violent tendencies, severely stressed about something, and holding scissors. Lucy sat down across from me, with her legs spread out before her like a young girl. Aaron finally came over and knelt to the left of us. He smiled at me, and I flashed him another angry look before turning my attention to Lucy.

"I'll tell you what you need to tell others," Lucy said. "But you need evidence first, Summer. No one will believe it otherwise."

"Evidence? You want me to get evidence?" I asked. "Evidence of what?"

"Of what Dr Rears has done, silly!" Lucy laughed her high-pitched giggle again.

"What has he done, though, Lucy? You haven't told me yet," I said.

It was the wrong thing to say. Her face darkened. She changed right in front of me, back to the colder version of Lucy.

The one from my dream. "Don't you know?" she growled at me.

Aaron noticed the change, and I saw his body tense. He looked ready to pounce if he needed to. Now that he was closer to me, I could see a trickle of blood rolling down the side of his face.

"Lucy," he said in a gentle voice, "of course, Summer knows. She wants to make sure she isn't missing anything."

I buried an urge to shout and scream and ask them what the fuck were they talking about. Thank God I was so used to strange situations. I pulled the face I always pulled when a patient was making no sense to me and at risk of becoming violent. I kept my expression blank, bar a small, encouraging smile.

"Oh!" Lucy giggled again and put her hand to her cheek. She had shifted back to the young girl routine again. "Of course! Silly me. Now, to get the evidence, you need to go to Dr Rears—"

Lucy didn't get to finish her sentence. The heavy metal door in the far right of the room burst open.

"She's in here!" A male voice boomed, shining his torch right at us.

We all winced at the light and covered our faces. The man stormed over, and two more men ran in after him. I could see their uniforms now. Aaron stood and immediately held both of his hands up in the air. The first police officer grabbed him and pushed him up against the wall, twisting his hands behind his back. He had obviously wrongly assumed that the male was the most dangerous person in the room, not the small woman opposite me still holding the scissors. Lucy jumped up and ran to the far corner, waving the scissors in front of her.

"Whoa," the second officer said. "It's okay, miss. No need to wave scissors around. We're here to check you're okay."

A third officer approached me, walking sideways so he could keep his eye on Lucy.

"Are you okay, miss? Can you stand?" He offered a hand to pull me up, and I took it gratefully.

"Yes, I think so. My head hurts," I replied.

Two more people came striding into the room. One was a female this time, the other male. They wore suits rather than police uniforms but had what I assumed to be some sort of police ID hanging around their necks. I guessed they were detectives, judging purely from movies I'd seen. The officer who had spoken to Lucy held his arm out to his side, motioning for the two suits to stop and stand still.

"Easy now," he said to them. "We have a lady here who is scared." He gestured towards Lucy.

I assumed *scared* was like the hospital version of *poorly*.

"Okay," the petite woman in the suit barked in an authoritative voice, belying her small stature. She didn't take her eyes off Lucy. "We'll take it from here. Get the others out."

The uniformed officer moved back a few paces as the suits slowly moved forward. The officer next to me held my arm, and we began to ease towards the door. Aaron was being walked out by the first officer.

"There's nowhere to go," the female suit said in the same bossy tone to Lucy. "Put the scissors down and come with us. We want to talk."

Lucy sobbed. She opened the scissors and held a sharp blade to her own throat. "Summer! Tell them." I couldn't help but turn around. Lucy looked at me, her eyes pleading.

"Tell us what?" the lady commanded without taking her eyes off Lucy. The male suit hadn't said a word but glanced over at me. He dwarfed the woman. He even dwarfed Aaron.

"Er…I'm not sure…" I stammered, looking at the man.

Lucy's sobs became anguished now. "You promised, you promised, you promised." She repeated over and over, getting louder and louder. The blade pushed into her neck, and a small trickle of blood ran down to Lucy's chest.

The suit lady tried again. "Hey, lady, scissors down, please."

I rolled my eyes. Jeez, she was going to get nowhere with that attitude.

"Lucy," I said in my own much calmer, authoritative voice, "I promised."

Lucy stopped bawling enough to look at me and listen. She still took deep breaths, as though it was difficult not to let the tears flow. She reminded me of times when Joshua had hurt himself but wanted to show he was a brave big boy.

"So I'm going to go with these nice police officers and tell them everything you've told me." I tried to reassure her.

"Tell them now!" she screamed at me. The scissors dug deeper, more blood trickled.

"But then it wouldn't be recorded!" I said in mock exasperation.

Lucy stared at me for a moment in silence. Her loud breaths had stopped and she cocked her head, before a wide grin spread across her face. Her child-like giggle escaped again. I knew I'd be hearing that laugh in my sleep.

"Oh! Goodie! Thanks, Summer!" she said through her laughter. The suits looked utterly flustered now.

"That's okay. I'm your advocate, aren't I? Now put the scissors down."

Lucy's face changed again. She looked at the suits. She could see by their baffled faces the effect she was having on them. Her lips curled into a smile. But not the young girl routine. An evil smile. It reminded me of when I saw her in the corridor, before she went missing.

"Lucy, I won't tell them if you don't put the scissors down right now," I said more sternly than I usually would have. Even I had my limits. She looked at me, smiled sweetly, and lowered the scissors to the floor as slowly as possible. The two uniformed officers who had been standing behind the suits ran at her with lightning speed. They pushed her up against the wall, dragging her arms behind her back as they had done with Aaron. Lucy howled out in pain. As awful as her screams were, I rushed out of the room as quickly as I could, with tears running down my face. I'm almost ashamed to say they weren't for Lucy. They were tears of relief. I was free. They had caught Lucy. I was safe. Joshua was safe. It was all going to be okay.

30

Summer

The bright lights of the hospital bored into my skull as I surveyed my surroundings. I sat in the emergency room of Derby City Hospital in a row of uncomfortable plastic chairs, with my back firmly against the wall. I knew Lucy wasn't there, but it would be a while before I turned my back on anyone again. One of the uniformed officers sat next to me. I'd since found out his name was PC Townsend. He didn't look like a cop. He was too skinny and not much taller than me. He was far too friendly, and had barely stopped talking on the way to the hospital. Thank God it was a five-minute drive. Though he was finally quiet, reading a fishing magazine he had picked up from the table in front of us.

I had since learned that Lucy held me captive in a rarely used storage room off the car park. She had been staying there since Friday. I'd noticed a sleeping bag and some other paraphernalia dotted around on my way out. I struggled to believe it had been three nights since she had gone missing. It felt more like months had passed. I'd also learned from PC

Townsend that Kelly was responsible for saving me. In all the drama, I had forgotten all about calling her to meet me. I was so grateful I had. Thanks to the storage room not being too far away, it took around an hour for the police to find me.

I was thankful that the emergency room wasn't too busy patient-wise. There were five other people in the waiting room. I normally loved to watch people, but not today. Nurses, doctors, and porters ran around me, pushing in and out of noisy doors. I hadn't spoken to Aaron so I was still unsure how much of Lucy's plan he was in on. His head had been bleeding, too. Surely he hadn't realised that Lucy was going to attack me. I couldn't understand why he would let me get hurt. *But then why not talk to me on the phone? Why did he lead me to the car park? Did he not see her sneaking up behind me?*

Yet, he knew Lucy was there. He obviously wanted me to see her. And he'd allowed her to hit me and tie me up, no matter what way I looked at it. I yearned for Joshua. My mum was still looking after him for me. It was the first thing I'd asked once Lucy was arrested. She and Joshua were both fine, other than my mum worrying about me. PC Townsend had said this as if it was obvious she would be concerned. I doubted she was that bothered.

I was so deep in thought it took a few seconds to register a woman calling my name. I looked up to see a young nurse smiling in our direction. PC Townsend told me he'd wait for me in the chair. He would give me a lift to the station once I was sorted. The nurse walked me into a small private room with two chairs on either side of a desk. She sat facing the huge old-style computer screen whilst I sat down in the opposite chair. I explained to her what had happened. Not the full story, but that I got hit in the back of the head with a blunt object by a mentally ill woman. She made the usual sympathetic noises without asking too many questions. She didn't seem too surprised. I guessed being an emergency room nurse she had heard stranger tales and likely dealt with many mentally ill patients. I'd had to call the emergency services a few times for patients in my previous role as support worker.

She took me through the standard head injury questions and tests. She shone a torch in my eyes, made me follow her finger, and took my temperature. Luckily, it didn't take long for her to decide I was okay. She wrapped up my wound and declared I could leave as long as I called my doctor or the emergency services if any of my symptoms changed. I promised I would and thanked her, grateful it was over so quickly.

It was when I was leaving that something strange happened. I made my way back down the corridor to the waiting room. As I reached PC Townsend, a figure outside the entrance to the emergency room caught my eye. Something about the person made my head snap around to get a better look. They wore dark trousers, a dark jumper, and had slicked black hair. I couldn't distinguish the facial features from where I stood, but I knew on some deep level that it was the same person who had been outside the cafe. Yet this time, I knew it couldn't be Lucy. *So who was it?*

31

Three. Four. I'm knocking...

Summer's silhouette was blurred as I watched her through the glass panelled entrance doors. She was sitting next to some skinny police officer. Though I couldn't enter because she would see me, and that couldn't happen yet. My plan wasn't quite ready, but it would have to do as it was, thanks to Aaron. I couldn't believe he had betrayed me. What an idiot. He was a spineless, diseased waste of space. He obviously didn't care about people as much as I thought he did. Unless maybe he didn't believe me. Maybe he didn't think I'd go through with it. Never mind, I had a plan to scare him. I knew how to show him I meant business. Aaron wouldn't tell the police about me, anyway. I was sure of it. He would have done it already if he had the balls.

Lucy probably would tell the police, but no one would believe that hot mess. She was a disgusting child killer. No one cared about child killers. No one cared about most of the patients. But an advocate? Aaron might tell *her*. And she might tell the police. I smiled as I watched her sit and stare at nothing. She looked pale and exhausted. Lucy had inadvertently helped me to start wearing her down. I squinted my eyes to get a good look at her injury. I couldn't see the wound, but I could make out blood around her head. My stomach fluttered as I thought about hurting her myself. I'd waited twenty years for revenge and I was now so close I could smell it. Her hair was dark and matted above her ear, and dry blood lined the neck of her ugly white top. Well done, Lucy, you psycho bitch. You made yourself even less believable.

She disappeared off down a corridor, following a nurse. I waited, enjoying that she looked so pathetic. I'd wait for thirty minutes. If she wasn't back by then, I'd go to her flat. Twenty minutes later, she returned. As she reached the cop again, she looked over at me. For once, I didn't move. I couldn't. The pull to see the same fear I'd witnessed outside the cafe was exhilarating, and I needed more of it.

She looked straight at me, but I couldn't tell if she recognised me. Her facial expression gave nothing away. In all the time I'd known her, it never had. But I knew her better than she knew herself. I had my gift, and I could see fear all over her face. I wanted to grab her, smell her fear, and tell her everything I knew about her. But then the plan would be even more screwed up. I needed to tear myself away. She turned away as the cop spoke to her, drawing her attention. I took my chance to sneak away. It wouldn't be goodbye for long, though. I would see Summer soon, and then she would disappear and Joshua would be mine.

32

Summer

I inwardly cursed PC Townsend for pulling my attention away from the staring figure. He'd only asked if I was okay, yet when I looked back a second later, they had disappeared.

"Sorry? Yes, I'm fine," I said.

PC Townsend hadn't moved from his seat and he looked up at me with concerned eyes. It was clear I hadn't convinced him I was fine. I smiled at him, and his expression relaxed.

"If you're feeling okay, are you happy to come over to the station with me? I'll drop you off at your car if you like, and you can follow me down. Or I can drive you there if you're not up for driving yet..." He trailed off as he stood up.

"Sure. I feel fine. Do you not need my car for forensics?" I instantly blushed when I saw him trying to hide a smirk.

"Not in this case. We could see from the camera that she didn't touch the car and we have all the photos we need. We've found you, got the suspect, and caught the whole thing on camera. There aren't any other forensics to obtain at this point."

I nodded. I wasn't sure if I should be driving, but I was too desperate for some time alone with my own thoughts to care. I needed to think about what I was going to tell the police. The truth, obviously, but I didn't want to be carted off to the hospital with Lucy. And I needed to figure out who the hell had been watching me. I was *not* going to raise that with the police.

I still hadn't moved, so PC Townsend took the lead and headed towards the hospital exit. The same doors that the figure had been standing behind. I convinced myself that nothing would happen while I was with a police officer and forced my feet forward to follow him. As we exited the hospital I pulled my coat up further around my shoulders to block out the harsh air. Winter was approaching, and leaves crunched under our feet as we walked. My gaze roamed the hospital grounds, but the mysterious figure had disappeared yet again, like a damn ghost. I stood still, trying to figure out where they could have gone. A separate department building flanked the emergency room on either side. Cars, trees, and other hospital buildings surrounded me in every direction. She could have disappeared into any one of them.

"Who are you looking for?" PC Townsend called out. He was about fifteen feet in front of me, standing by his police car. He was more perceptive than he looked.

"No one," I said. He raised an eyebrow. "Well, I wondered what happened to Aaron? Did he come to the hospital?"

"Oh!" He was livelier then, his arms moving everywhere as he spoke. "No, he refused hospital treatment. I reckon he's still at the station. He'll at least be answering questions, I assume."

"Will you charge him with anything?"

"Did he do anything illegal?" he asked. I'd forgotten PC

Townsend didn't actually know what had happened at this point. He knew less than I did.

"Erm, I'm not really sure." I told a partial truth. I wished I could have spoken to Aaron before I had to give my statement to the police, but I knew that wouldn't happen.

I crunched through more noisy leaves as I joined PC Townsend at his squad car. He opened the door for me so I could climb into the back seat, and set off on the short drive back to my car in the supermarket car park. He smiled at me once he was in the front seat, but didn't say another word. I'd been in the back of a police car on one other occasion. The drive reminded me of that day and the last incident with my elder brother. The police had given me a lift home, and Eddie's girlfriend, Marinda, had sat next to me. She'd been my appropriate adult when they questioned me. She'd told me not to say anything to get my brother in trouble but I told them everything I knew. I hadn't seen Marinda since. My mum had been in no fit state to tell them anything. He'd nearly killed her. The memory of what my brother had done made me feel nauseous. The panic I'd felt, and all the blood. I'd seen the nightmare unfold as I hid under the rickety table in the kitchen corner, whispering down the phone to the emergency services lady. Eddie had thought I'd been to school, but I'd been off sick. For a moment, I wished I had an appropriate adult in the car with me. Kelly, or maybe even my mum, would do. I was fed up with being alone and always the appropriate adult. I was constantly scared of being unable to protect Joshua. It was exhausting.

Anxiety pulled at my stomach as the car slowed and we entered the dark space. I closed my eyes until we rolled to a stop. When I opened them, PC Townsend was already getting out of the car. He came to my side to open the door for me and held out his hand to help me out. I had an urge to bat it away, but managed to control myself and take his hand. My car was only a few feet away, but he walked by my side as we made our way over. I assumed he could sense my apprehension and my cheeks coloured at the thought.

"Don't worry. I'll be fine getting in." I smiled at him.

"Okay." He smiled back and walked back to his car. I jumped into the driver's seat before he disappeared from view. I didn't actually want to be alone there.

As I sat in my car, the anxiety dissipated. Being in my own surroundings and in control of the vehicle made me feel stronger. I shook away the ridiculous feeling of wanting company. Joshua and I were better off alone. Only the police to talk to, and then I could be with him again. I just hoped that the figure from the hospital stayed away.

33

Summer

The grey walls of the police station interview room were the opposite of the bright white walls of Derby Hospital. The two suits from the storage room of the underground car park were seated in front of me. I'd found out that the broad man was DI Alex Swanson. The bossy woman was DI Rebecca Hart. The name did not suit her personality from what I had seen of her.

Swanson hadn't spoken much, but he focused his deep brown eyes directly on me. I shifted uncomfortably in the hard chair. Not because he stared, but because he looked as though he was trying to figure me out, and there was something about him that made me believe he would succeed. Though his thick beard made it somewhat difficult to tell what he was thinking.

"So, Summer. Are you feeling well enough to talk to us?" she asked. Her short brown bob moved in line with her chin as she looked up. She gave off an air of being in control.

I struggled to tear my eyes away from him as Hart spoke. His suit defied his lumberjack structure, like he'd be more comfortable in a gym. I decided not to look at him again and focussed on Hart's perfectly symmetrical face instead.

"Yes. Yes, I do," I replied.

My eyes flicked straight back to Swanson. He had more hair on his face than on his head, which wasn't difficult to accomplish. I forced myself to turn away again, but I could still feel his intense stare.

"Let's start with how you know Lucy Clarke." She glanced up at me and smiled briefly before looking back down at her notepad. She looked at Swanson, then at the floor, then back at me. I couldn't tell if she was impatient or distracted.

"I'm her advocate," I replied. Hart looked blankly at me, so I explained further. "I work for Rowan Advocacy as an Independent Mental Health Advocate. Lucy resides on Bluebell Ward in Derby Hospital. I visit the ward twice a week as an independent person for patients to speak to."

"So you speak to all the patients on Bluebell Ward?" Hart asked. "I thought advocates were like lawyers? Available by appointment?"

"No, I visit twice a week and sit on the ward for an hour or so. Patients choose whether they want to speak to me. They don't have to, but they do all legally need to have access to someone like me. The advocates by appointment tend to be council advocates not employed privately like me."

Hart nodded. "Did you know Lucy was no longer on Bluebell Ward?"

"Yes. I didn't know where she was..." I trailed off, unsure what to say next. "When I asked the staff, they weren't sure who I meant."

"They didn't know who you meant?" Hart looked at me incredulously. I knew how she felt. "How do they not know their own patients?"

"I'm not sure. I've been trying to find out but have not had much luck. I'd spoken to Dr Rears and Aaron, who you met earlier. Then Aaron rang me today and said he had something to tell me about Lucy and asked me to meet him at the car park. But then Lucy hit me…I think." I trailed off and looked back at Swanson. He was still intently focused on me, and I felt my cheeks blush. I was babbling.

"So she was with you and Aaron? Why did she hit you?" Hart asked.

"Well, I don't know to be honest. She wasn't there at first. It was Aaron and me talking. Then I heard a noise, and someone hit me. I woke up in that room, and I was tied up with zip wire. That's why she had scissors. She had cut me free. She wanted to tell me something about Dr Rears. She seemed to want to check if she could trust me before she told me."

"By knocking you out and tying you up?"

"Well, she isn't very well." I shrugged my shoulders. I'd seen stranger things happen. I'm sure these two had, too.

"Hmm. That's one way, I suppose. So what did she tell you?" Hart responded.

"She kept talking about Dr Rears, the consultant psychiatrist from the hospital. She said he is bad and I need to tell people. But she didn't say exactly what he's done."

"Patients from there tell the police all sorts." Hart rolled her eyes. "We'll see what she tells us."

"What will happen to her? To Lucy, I mean?"

"Well, she'll go back to the hospital. She's under their care,"

"No!" The word came out far louder than I had meant to say it. I rubbed my face in my hands and took a deep breath to regain my calm. "I mean, she can't go back to a place where she is being abused."

"We don't know that she is being abused. We get calls from the hospital all the time. The patients tell us they're being held against their will, physically beaten etc, etc. It's never true. It's their illness." Hart shrugged again.

"It doesn't matter if it's true." I sounded snotty, but I couldn't help it. "She believes it. Can't you imagine how scary that is for her?"

"Yes, but helping her with that isn't our job. That's her doctor's job." Hart crossed her arms and glared at me. I should have stayed calm.

"The same person she believes is abusing her?" I tried to sound less snotty, but I was pretty sure it hadn't worked.

"Yes, but even if she changes hospitals and doctors, she'll say the same thing, won't she? She is ill."

"As long as I've known her, Lucy has never accused anyone of abuse."

"How long have you known her?"

"Six months."

Hart made a snorting noise through her nose. "That's not that long." She reminded me of Joshua when he tried to win an argument. I decided that I'd had enough of the woman.

"What do you think?" I directed my question to Swanson. At least then, I could legitimately look at him without it seeming weird.

He shrugged his large shoulders and cast a glance over to Hart. They shared a look, and I briefly wondered if they'd ever had sex. Jealousy pinged at my chest. I knew it was ridiculous. I didn't know the guy at all.

"Like DI Hart says, we aren't mental health experts," he finally said.

I'd heard enough. I put my hand to my head then, feigning

pain. "I need to go home. I need to—"

"We do have more questions for you." Hart interrupted.

"I need to get my son." I stood as if she hadn't spoken. I knew my rights and wasn't going to be bullied by this unempathetic nightmare.

"Oh, okay. Please give us your contact details. We will be in touch soon then," she mumbled.

I gave them my contact details and rushed out of the room. Swanson followed me to unlock the outside corridor door. As we walked along, side by side, I forced myself to look straight ahead. But we stopped before the locked door and he looked down at me, keys in his hand.

"Miss Thomas, have you called me this week?"

Oh shit. I realised then that this was the guy who that receptionist had put me through to earlier in the day. He believed I was some sort of lunatic who had been calling nonstop about Lucy.

"I called the station once today, and that was it," I said more sternly than I had expected too.

He studied me for a moment before asking, "Who do you think called me pretending to be you then?"

I paused before answering, unsure how to respond. "Well, maybe it was Lucy. Maybe she wanted to be found," I replied eventually. He nodded and unlocked the door to allow me to leave.

The autumn sun cut into my eyes as it set for the evening. It must have been around 6 PM. I raised my hand across my forehead to block it out as I rushed to the car. I didn't want to be out in the dark.

A shadow moved in the far corner of the car park. *Was that a person? A small animal? Was I being watched again?* I froze in the middle of the car park and peered in the shadow's direction. A painfully cold breeze hit my face, but I stayed as still as a statue. There was nothing there. *Was I actually losing my mind?*

I raced forward again towards my car and heard footsteps approaching behind me. I whipped around and stepped back, hands up to defend myself this time. She would not get me again. My breath whooshed out of me as I saw Swanson striding towards me.

"Sorry…didn't mean to scare you…" He trailed off as he reached me, eyeing at me in the same intense way he had done inside the interview room. I suddenly realised why he was so familiar to me. He observed me in the same way I observe others. He was calm and unreadable, too. We were the same, maybe we were connected. I wondered if he felt the same. I had a sudden impulse to let go of my emotions. To unleash my misery upon this man I barely knew. To hug him tight and beg him to protect Joshua and me.

"You didn't scare me." I lied instead. It was such a foolish lie. He had clearly scared me half to death.

"I wanted to make sure you're okay. You've had a rough day." His expression changed, and he almost smiled.

"I'm fine." I lied again. I didn't smile back.

"Okay. Well, if you need anything, here's my card." He handed me a small card with his name, division, and work number on it. I could have hugged him. Maybe he saw me, too.

"Thanks, but I doubt I will need it." I instantly regretted being so unpleasant.

"That's fine." He shrugged off my arrogance and smiled properly.

Every bone in my body wanted to stay close to him, but I

turned and walked to my car. He watched me as I went, and I had to fight the compulsion to turn back to him. Sometimes, I really should listen to my intuition.

34

Swanson

Once Summer had driven off, Swanson made his way back to the station to collect Hart. They needed to get to the custody suite on the other side of town to speak to Lucy. Hopefully, she was calm enough. They had already spoken to Aaron while Summer was in the hospital. Swanson didn't know what to make of him. He was some sort of modern hippy man. He wore jeans that were ridiculously tight and looked stupid. There was a hole in his ear the size of a two pence coin and dark makeup smudged around his eyes. To each their own, but Swanson wouldn't be caught dead looking like that.

It was obvious that Aaron hadn't told them everything he knew. His story was that Lucy had somehow escaped, found out where he lived and followed him to the car park. Swanson had seen the camera footage from the car park before finding Summer. It was grainy and flickered, but it showed Aaron and Summer talking. It was like watching an old horror movie with no sound. He'd watched a flickering, grey Lucy crawling around a nearby car before creeping up to Summer with an object in her hand. She'd stood just behind Summer and whacked her so hard she fell like a sack of spuds.

Aaron had run over and knelt by Summer, but as there was no sound, they couldn't hear what was being said. After a minute or so of Aaron and Lucy speaking and waving their arms around at each other, Lucy began pointing in the direction of the storeroom. Aaron and Lucy then picked Summer up and walked off-camera. No cameras were pointing at the storage room, but it hadn't been too hard to find once they'd watched the footage. Aaron told them Lucy was living in the storage room and she said she had a first aid kit there. In his panic he hadn't thought that firstly, this was a lie because why would Lucy have a first aid kit? And secondly, it would be infinitely easier to bring the first aid kit to Summer rather than carry her dead weight all the way there. However, once they were there, as he laid Summer down, Lucy had taken the opportunity to knock him out as well. In his defence, he had clearly been whacked on the head with something pretty hard, though he'd refused hospital treatment. Neither Swanson nor Hart believed Aaron's reason for dragging Summer to the storage room. But they'd let him go home for now with a warning to stay away from both Summer and Lucy.

Swanson reached the station doors and noted that Hart was waiting for him on the other side. She caught his eye and raised an eyebrow. He nodded in return, signalling for her to come outside. He walked towards his car and jumped into the driver's side to start it up whilst he waited for her, and flicked on the heating to warm his icy hands. Hart joined him a minute later and he pulled out of the car park, headed for the custody suite.

"So, what do you think of her, then?" Hart asked, peering

out the front passenger window. Rain began to drizzle down the glass, giving a distorted view of objects and people as they drove through town.

"I don't know. The whole situation is fucked up. It's pissing me off." Swanson's forehead was wrinkled in frustration. He'd had this feeling many times before, but this case was stranger than most. "I don't think it was her that called earlier this week. I think *she* called today, which is what she told me when I walked her out,"

"Then who has been calling? Lucy herself, maybe?"

"That's my bet. She wanted to communicate but maybe wasn't sure how."

"What gets me is the hospital not reporting her missing," Hart said.

"It's not that they didn't report it. They didn't admit it. I spoke to them myself. That doctor said he didn't *have* any patients called Lucy. Now that's weird."

Hart nodded her head in agreement, but they both fell silent, lost in their thoughts. They pulled up at the custody suite soon after and hurried inside to get out of the now pouring rain. A few minutes later, they were sitting outside the interview room waiting for an officer to bring Lucy to them and introduce them. With Lucy being ill, they had to tread carefully. The door banged shut as another officer walked through and approached them.

"Hi, guys. You're not speaking to Lucy tonight, I'm afraid. We're still trying to contact her doctor to get the medication she needs, and she has no legal support yet or an appropriate adult."

"Can we not get someone in as an emergency?" Swanson asked.

The officer shrugged. "It won't make a difference until we can get her meds."

Hart gave the officer a foul look as if it were his fault. The officer stared steadily back at her.

"Fine," Swanson muttered as he turned to leave.

"Where next?" Hart asked as they walked out of the custody suite. "The doctor?"

Swanson thought for a moment as he stood at the top of the steps where the rain couldn't reach them thanks to a roof overhang. Then he remembered the other event that didn't add up.

"The friend," he said.

Hart cocked her head for a moment before realising what he meant. "The friend who drove to the mum's house before calling the police?" She smiled.

Swanson nodded. "Yep, that friend. Let's see what she has to say about not calling the police straight away."

35

Summer

I sat in my mum's kitchen with my stiff fingers gripping a hot cup of sweet tea. It was disgusting, but it was helping with the shaking. The heat seared through my hands, and I was starting to feel them again. For the first time since Dad had died, I was comforted by being in my mum's environment. I felt safe with the scribbled drawings on the fridge, the rickety chair I was sitting in, and even the pictures of my brothers and me dotting the walls. Joshua would be back soon, and I couldn't wait. Mum had taken him to the park, but they were due to return at any minute. Lucy was locked away. Whether she was in the police station or the hospital, I didn't know, but I knew someone had incarcerated her somewhere, and she couldn't get to us. *So who'd been watching me at the hospital?*

I texted Kelly to confirm I was fine and would call her soon. I'd had thirty-three missed calls from her in her panic to find me. Lucy's marred face still played in my mind. She had been so desperate for me to help her, and I *wanted* to help her. I hated the thought of her going back to Dr Rears. If I was honest, it wasn't Lucy's desperate plea that convinced me she wasn't lying. I hated to admit it, but Hart was right when she said unfounded accusations happened all the time. It was Dr Rears himself. It was the way he drew his eyes over the younger female patients. The way he taught staff to have an *us* and *them* attitude. The simple way he had lied about Lucy not even existing. He was a liar and a pervert, so it wasn't a huge jump to believe Lucy when she called him an abuser. I made a promise to Lucy to help her, and I meant it. I also needed to know who was following me if it wasn't Lucy. To figure that out, I had to concentrate on helping Lucy. If I could get that part of the puzzle, then the rest would fit together. I hoped, anyway. It was all I could think to do and certainly beat doing nothing.

I'd borrowed a plain beige jumper from my mum's clean washing pile on the couch. I hadn't wanted Joshua to see the blood on my top. It was barely a few spots, but it was enough to be noticeable. I'd carefully washed my neck first, but there was nothing I could do about the padded bandage above my right ear. As long as he could see I was okay, he shouldn't be too startled by it. I'd tell him I'd simply fallen. Five minutes later, I heard the jangle of keys as Mum opened the front door. I stood, ready to show Joshua I was definitely okay despite the bandage. I heard his footsteps running into the entrance hall. He must have shoved past my mum as he came running through the door like a freight train. He wrapped his tiny arms around my waist as tight as he could. I held him as close as possible without cutting off his oxygen supply and kissed his head. I felt whole again with him in my arms. I was so focused on Joshua that I didn't notice my mum. To my shock, she was hot on his heels to embrace me. She didn't wait for a response but wrapped her arms around both of us. She sniffled, and I felt her tears on my cheek. I swallowed and bit back my own tears. I couldn't remember the last time I'd hugged her. If she had tried last week, I might have run away. But now I didn't want her to let go.

Joshua laughed. "Group hug!" he shouted, making both Mum and I laugh along with him. Tears still threatened to escape, so I stood up straight to release their grip and gather myself.

"I guess you both missed me then!" I looked at my mum. Tears were flowing down her cheeks. She smiled at me before walking out into the corridor. I assumed to collect herself so Joshua wouldn't see her tears. I felt an urge to follow her but turned my attention back to Joshua instead. He needed me more.

"Yes! I missed you a million gazillion times!" he shouted up at me with his skinny arms still locked around my waist. "I missed you more than you missed me!"

Everything was a competition with this kid. I laughed again. I'd missed him trying to outdo me.

"Not possible," I told him and squeezed my arms around him again. When I let go, he finally released me. I sat back down, and he kept a hand on my leg. I wasn't going anywhere if he could help it.

"How was the park?" I asked.

"Great! Mamma went down the slide and got stuck!" He laughed, showing his gappy smile, where his front tooth had fallen out a few days ago.

"Oh, I'd better check on her!" I said, squeezing his hand as I stood again. "Go into the lounge and put some TV on."

He eyed me carefully. "Okay. I'll be right there." He pointed at the couch. "Don't go anywhere?"

I smiled and reassured him I wasn't going anywhere. It seemed to help as he skipped away to put on his current favourite show about dinosaurs. I wandered tentatively into the hallway in search of Mum. She was leaving the downstairs toilet as I entered the corridor. Her face looked fresh now, and I wondered if maybe I'd imagined the tears. I hadn't imagined the hug, though. I smiled at her.

"Are you okay, Mum?" I asked, not sure what else to say. She grimaced and looked as though she might break down again.

"Oh, Summer. I'm so glad you're okay. I was so scared when that lady came round to say you were missing."

"It's okay, Mum. It was an escaped patient from work. She wasn't actually trying to hurt me. She wanted my help."

"You need to stop working with these people. You need to work somewhere safer. Mandy said there's a job going at the old folks' home. You could look after them instead. It's basically the same thing."

"I'm fine, Mum." I tried again, but she continued.

"You don't have to do it, though, Summer. You don't owe Eddie anything." She let her words hang in the air. Her face fell as though she was scared she'd said the wrong thing and made me angry.

"I know," it was all I could manage to say. We hadn't spoken about Eddie since I had failed to find him or Marinda over a decade ago. Mum had wanted me to stay away, so that conversation hadn't ended well. I did not want to argue with her right now. It was the closest we'd been in a long time and, after today, I felt a desire to protect her.

"Who told you I was missing?" I changed the subject instead. "DI Hart? That was quick. They found me within an hour, and Hart was with the police officers."

"Er, no. Your friend came round," she said. She looked away now, busying herself with organising the windowsill full of random knick knacks, including a nodding dog, an old silver clock, and some random papers.

"Do you mean Kelly?" I tried again.

"No, Kelly rang me later though through Facebook. It was your friend with black hair, tied up in a ponytail. She was about your height, a bit older than you, though."

Fear shot through me like I'd never felt before. There were two women I could think of with black hair. One was incarcerated. The other was following me, and now she knew where Joshua was.

36

Summer

There's a certain mode I always go into when Joshua is in danger. Like the time he fell from a ten-foot climbing frame in a park. Or when he got lost for less than a minute on the beach in Spain. I referred to it as *Mum Mode*. I never was any good at naming feelings despite my background. I didn't know if it was something that happened to all parents or not. There was no panic or fretting involved, as you'd probably expect from a distressed parent. It was a fear-driven sense of urgency, and business-like. I knew if I panicked, I wouldn't make good decisions, so I stayed terrifyingly calm. Every possible scenario and resolution flew through my mind in seconds. And I knew in less than a minute what I had to do.

For the first time since we had broken up, I called Richard and told him I needed his support. I explained what had happened with Lucy and asked him to have Joshua. I was unsure if Lucy was in custody and thought Joshua would be best off staying with him for the night while I sorted the situation. To my relief, he agreed instantly. Mum went to stay with my aunt, which she did at least once a fortnight, anyway. Again I didn't tell her the full story, and instead told her I thought that the girl who had visited claiming to be my friend was the patient's friend. She'd argued that I should go with her but eventually agreed to let me sort it. I barely listened to her as I helped her pack and waited for my aunt to arrive.

Joshua was even less impressed he couldn't go home with me but was excited to spend an extra night with his dad. I told him I needed to rest my head and would be back for him tomorrow, which he seemed to accept. I knelt at my mum's living room window, resting my knees on the frayed carpet. I peered through the glass, searching for any signs of the stranger with black hair. Mum had already gone and left me a spare key to lock up her front door.

It would be hard for anyone to hide on the quiet street outside. It was a narrow road with many semi-detached redbrick houses, and each had a short driveway, so there were few cars parked on the road. I had even parked my own car on Mum's drive today, wanting to be as close to the front door as possible. It was early evening so the sun had set, and the dull light of the street lamps was all I had to pick out a figure creeping in the darkness. I waited and watched for a few minutes, but I didn't see anyone. Joshua still sat on the sofa watching telly and ignoring my strange behaviour.

I casually walked outside under the pretence of vaping and wandered out past the drive to the tarmac pathway to look around. I had a hammer up the sleeve of the winter coat I'd borrowed from Mum. Luckily, she was a size bigger than me, so there was plenty of room to fit the weapon in without it looking obvious. The street was still quiet, the brisk autumn winds keeping most people in the warmth of their homes.

It was then or never. I had to risk it. I hurried back inside and told Joshua it was time to go. We walked back to the car together, holding hands. He chuntered excitedly as he clambered into the car.

"Mummy, did you know twelve times twelve is one hundred and forty-four? And that plants give out oxygen? They breathe in carbon dioxide and breathe out oxygen!" He dramatically breathed in and out as he spoke to show me what plants did. Then he grinned into the rear-view mirror, awaiting my appreciation of his newfound intelligence.

"Wow! That's amazing, baby. You're so clever." I smiled into the mirror as I made sure our doors were locked.

"I'm at Daddy's for *one* night though, right, Mummy? Then your head will be better?" His voice was full of concern.

"I think so, baby, yes." I didn't want to promise, but if all went to plan, it would all be over tomorrow.

Once he had clipped himself in, I took another look up and down the dark street. I still couldn't see anyone lurking, so I kicked the engine into gear and set off on the short drive to Richard's house. I kept expecting someone to jump out from behind a lamp post or driveway. Richard's house was five minutes from my mum's, but I kept my eye out for any cars that seemed to be going in the same direction. To my relief, the roads were quiet. A red car sat behind me for a couple of turns, but it pulled off not long before Richard's turn. There were no cars behind me when I turned into his street. I pulled up to the house and decided to get out and walk Joshua to the door instead of phoning Richard. I wanted to make sure no one was lurking around and watching us. Richard looked surprised to see me at the door with Joshua. I didn't blame him, seeing as I normally stayed in the car.

"Hey, you okay?" His voice was strained, as though he felt more awkward than usual.

"I'm fine." I was getting sick of saying that.

"Hi, Daddy. Bye, Mummy. Love you more." Joshua gave me a big squeeze before he ran past his dad and into the house.

"He's had chicken nuggets for tea and been to the park, so should be fairly tired," I told Richard. "I'll get him tomorrow at dinner time if you're okay to pick him up from school, please?"

"Yeah, that's fine. See you tomorrow."

"Bye." I gave an awkward half-smile and turned to walk back to my car.

"Summer?" Richard called after me. I turned back around. He stared at me, seemingly forgetting what he was going to say. "If you need anything, call me." He finally blurted out.

I didn't bother pointing out that I had already called him for help. I got what he was saying. As much as I appreciated the gesture, I couldn't help a gremlin of annoyance flaring up within me. I didn't want Richard to think I needed him. I didn't need him. Joshua did. There was a difference.

"Will do," I said as I continued to walk away.

Back in the car, I wondered where to go. *Did I go home? Was it safe?* I thought about calling Kelly, but I didn't want to drag her into the situation any further. If I was not safe, then surely anyone around me wasn't safe, either. I took out my phone and looked online. There was a hotel down the road from me at forty quid for the night. I booked it immediately and drove right there, stopping off at the supermarket on the way for clean underwear and a cheap outfit. It would all be over tomorrow. As long as I followed the plan.

37

Summer

I awoke to a deep nagging pain above my right ear the next morning, courtesy of the previous day's attack. I grimaced as I carefully opened my eyes. Unfamiliar, white-washed walls enveloped me. They looked exactly like the walls on the Bluebell Ward. Panic grabbed at me as I sat up in bed and threw off the covers. *Had they carted me off to the ward?*

But as the rest of my surroundings gradually registered—the desk phone on the bedside table, the flatscreen TV on the wall, the bright purple armchair in the room's corner—the memory of checking into the hotel came back to me. I had spent so little time in the room before falling into a deep sleep. I wasn't sure if it was from exhaustion or the bang to the head, but it was the best night's sleep I'd had since last week.

An uneasy feeling overcame me as I remembered what I had to do that day. I grabbed my phone from under my pillow to text Richard, wanting to make sure Joshua was okay before anything else. I held my fingerprint on the lock screen to wake it up and saw I had three missed calls from Aaron. I glared at the phone and tutted, as if Aaron could see my reaction. I ignored his calls and sent the text to Richard. I had things to do and needed to get to work. I needed to shower and get ready to pretend everything was normal.

I had managed to wash the blood out of my hair last night before collapsing on the bed. So I tied it into a tight bun to shower, I pulled on the new khaki trousers and light grey blouse I'd purchased the night before, and slipped on my thick-heeled black ankle boots, grateful I'd had them with me. They were easy to run in and would be great for kicking someone should I need to. Again I added some makeup, just a bit of what I kept in my handbag. Foundation, blusher, mascara, and lip gloss before finishing with a spritz of perfume. I didn't remember ever putting perfume in my bag but was glad it was there.

I grabbed my laptop bag and keys before striding out of the hotel room and down the three flights of stairs. I ignored the elevator. They were horrible, claustrophobic things. It was barely 8 AM, yet the hotel was busy. Mostly with people in business-type suits waiting for breakfast or their taxis. Nobody paid much attention to me as I dropped my hotel room key into the check-out box and made my way through the exit. Icy air slapped my face as I strode confidently to the car. I'd parked as close to the entrance doors as I could get. I picked up my pace with each step, eager for the day to be over. Today was the day I would get evidence for Lucy and make sure Joshua was safe.

I slid into the front seat of the car, slamming and locking the door behind me. Anxiety had begun to manifest as a dense pit of nausea at the bottom of my stomach. I breathed in deeply until I could inhale no more and held my breath for ten seconds before releasing. My patients found it useful when they were stressed, and I could see why. I will do this for Lucy and for Joshua, I told myself as I repeated the breathing exercise. I clicked the seatbelt and put the car in gear, manoeuvring out of the car park and down the dual carriageway to the hospital. Once on the road, my anxiety was replaced by determination.

The characterless brickwork of the hospital came into sight not long after I took the exit from the dual carriageway. I swung into the car park and reversed into a spot in the far corner. I snuck into the back seat of my car. From there, the large entrance was in my eye line, but it was difficult for anyone to see me. My anxiety rose further with each passing minute as I sat, unmoving, for about half an hour. I forced it back down, using the same technique I'd used earlier. Doubt made me reconsider what I was doing. *Should I walk away? Should I call Swanson?*

A loud ringing startled me out of my thoughts. I looked at my phone to see that Aaron was calling. I was wondering whether to answer when a noise made my head snap up. The familiar sound of Dr Rears's rambunctious laugh was close by. He had appeared by the entrance alongside a patient. My heart sank. It was sweet, anxiety-riddled Louise. *Was that how she had gotten him to agree to unsupervised leave? By promising to go somewhere with him?*

Louise was grinning from ear to ear, excitement radiating from her. A need to protect her overtook my anxiety. My maternal instinct reached out for her, and it was stronger than my fear. I climbed carefully back into the front seat, cursing the gear stick as I did so, and switched on the ignition. My phone had stopped ringing so I raised it to snap some pictures of Dr Rears and Louise together, trying to get the evidence

Lucy and I needed. Dr Rears and Louise walked over to a new Audi parked right in front of the entrance. Dr Rears jumped into the driver's seat. I had expected Louise to join him, but to my surprise, she wandered off down the side path. It led off the hospital grounds and straight to the main road.

I had a split second to decide who to follow as Dr Rears pulled out of the car park. I knew Louise was safe if she wasn't with him, so I drove slowly after Dr Rears, staying well back. He turned right out of the car park, then right and right again onto the main road. The same way Louise had walked. He pulled off into a shop car park and unease hit me as I realised he was going to pick up Louise. She wasn't safe at all. I pulled over on the side of the road and waited. Sure enough, Louise came out of the shop a few seconds later and sat in the front passenger seat of the car. She was still beaming from ear to ear. Dr Rears must have promised her a nice day out. I felt sick at the thought of what he might do to her.

They left the car park, and I followed a few cars behind. Luckily, he didn't take many turns, so it was easy to keep up. We were in the busy city center, and there were lots of other cars to hide behind. The rain came back, which also made it harder for them to see me. I concentrated hard on his dark Audi for fear of losing them. Within a few minutes, he'd pulled onto the motorway. The unease grew deeper in my stomach as I realised they must be going to Edwinstowe. He was taking her to that creepy house. *How fucking dare he?* I prayed I was wrong, but they turned onto Coppice Court half an hour later. I didn't follow, choosing instead to park around the corner as I had before. I exited the car and stood behind a tree on the corner about two hundred feet away from them.

As she got out of the car, a look of uncertainty had replaced

Louise's beaming smile. A furious rage bubbled within me which I pushed down. I didn't need unhelpful emotions right now. I needed to stay calm. I needed evidence. I snapped a couple of quick pictures of the two of them entering his house. I waited, checking the time continually on my phone. Two minutes passed. Then five. Then ten. It felt so much longer. Thoughts of what he might do to Louise agitated me, making my impatience grow.

After ten minutes, I strolled towards the property, searching up and down the street as I did so. Still, I saw no one, and the street was quiet. No cars drove down the potholed road. No feet walked the crumbled pavement. No one hid behind any cars. I took my chance and picked up pace to the house. I stooped and hurried up the drive, using the Audi for cover. It occurred to me that if anyone saw me, I would look ridiculous.

Once I reached the grimy front of the property, I peered through the grease-streaked window. I could make out the back of Louise as she climbed the stairs. I watched and waited. It wasn't much above freezing outside, but beads of sweat had gathered on my forehead. I couldn't stand at the window for too long for fear a neighbour would call the police, though I got the impression that the police were not so welcome on this particular street. I stepped to the front door and nudged down the handle. It wasn't a heavy door and easily clicked open. The cocky bastard hadn't even locked it. My phone was still in my hand, and I lifted it, pressing the record button. I wondered if what I was doing was illegal. I hadn't broken in, so I hoped it wasn't. The door groaned as it opened, and the stench of rotten food greeted me. I held my breath and pushed the thoughts about going to prison out of my mind.

Poised to run if I needed to, I stood at the threshold silently, and strained my ears for signs that one of them had heard me, that someone was coming to check the noise, but there were none. I could hear the low rumbling of a male voice upstairs, though the words were indiscernible. Louise's laughter floated down too. A voice told me to run. Had it not been for Joshua, I probably would have listened. Thinking of Joshua pushed my frozen legs forward into the hallway. The dark carpet underfoot allowed me to creep silently to the bottom of the stairwell. I left the front door wide open, though. I couldn't bear the thought of being closed in, not inside that house.

As slowly as possible, I crept up the stairs. I stopped at each step to check if the rumbling voices had stopped, ready to run if someone came to check the noises. They didn't. They were oblivious to my sneaking around. I reached the top and stood still, not daring to move. A narrow landing loomed in front of me. Tiny pinpricks of anxiety electrified my body, and the urge to run away was beginning to win.

There was an open door to my left and another further down the corridor. I quickly side-stepped through the closest door to catch my breath. I tried to remember the task at hand, but my head was spinning too much to think straight. I pushed the door partially closed and hid behind it, leaning my forehead against the wall, unsure what to do now that I was inside. I needed to catch Dr Rears in the act, or it would all be for nothing. I breathed in deeply, once again attempting to drown the anxiety that threatened to overtake me. It didn't work. I took my head away from the wall, needing to get out. I needed to run. But I realised as I turned to make my escape, that it was too late. Dr Rears was standing in the doorway, staring straight at me.

38

Summer

There was barely a metre between us. I tried to move back, but my limbs wouldn't listen. He didn't move, either. His eyes and mouth were wide open as he gawked back at me. Silence electrified the air between us.

"Hellooo?" A woman's voice cut through the silence, breaking the spell we both seemed to be under. I managed to step back and create more distance between us. He did the same as Louise appeared in the doorway. She put her arms around Dr Rears neck, but he shrugged her off and nodded his head in my direction.

"Look who we have here," he rasped at her as if it was hard to talk. Then he smiled, suddenly as cheerful as ever.

"Summer?" Louise looked over and spotted me standing at the back of the room with my phone still pointing at them. She grinned at me. "What are you doing here?"

I opened my mouth to speak, but no words would come. A stupid grin in her direction was all I could manage. I was stupid to have gone inside the house. My mouth was stuck together, too dry to operate properly. I looked around the small room. My vision focused better. An instinct to get back to Joshua took my panic over.

"Louise…" The word was barely audible, and I cleared my throat to try again. "Can you get me some water, please?"

Louise threw me a confused look at my strange request, but ambled off down the stairs without saying a word. She hadn't appeared scared of Dr Rears. I couldn't understand why not if he had been abusing patients, as Lucy had suggested.

"Are you going to tell me what you are doing here, Summer?" Dr Rears looked at me smugly. "Breaking into my house?"

"I was going to ask you the same thing," I retorted. I couldn't believe the audacity that I could catch him with a patient alone in a random house, and he still made out like I was the one in the wrong. As if *he* was innocent. "This is not your house for one thing, and I saw you come in here from my friend's house. I saw Louise with you, and the front door was wide open, so there was no breaking in. If you'd like me to leave, I'd be happy to, but I caught it on camera." I raised my phone higher to make it clear I was still recording.

Dr Rears went pale, my words landing where I needed them to. He turned his back to me and stormed away. He'd turned left, so I knew he was still upstairs. I considered making a run for it. I listened with bated breath. I could hear clanging from the kitchen downstairs as Louise busied herself getting me some water, but nothing from wherever Dr Rears had gone. It occurred to me he might be fetching some sort of weapon.

"Hello? Yes, I'm at number twelve. I'll be back over in a minute. See you soon," I said loudly to nobody.

"Where are you going?" Louise appeared in the doorway, making my heart almost come through my chest. Jesus. I hadn't heard her coming.

"Oh, my friend is waiting for me." I quickly recovered.

She entered the room and passed me a tall glass of water. The glass was grubby as if it hadn't been washed for a while. I took it from her regardless and guzzled, the drum in my head subsiding.

"What's going on, Louise?" I whispered. Unsure now of where Dr Rears was and afraid of him coming back.

"Oh, this is Dr Rears' house." She was so blasé about the situation, not seeming to realise that what was happening was wrong. She beamed at me, her big brown eyes full of innocence despite the hardship she'd suffered at such a young age. This trip was an adventure for her.

"Okay, but why are you here, in this house?" I asked.

"Well, I'm on my leave, and you turned up!" She laughed loudly.

"Oh." I smiled at her. The haze in my mind was clearing now that Dr Rears was away from me. "I saw you guys from my friend's house and came round to say hi."

"Ohhhh." She nodded her head as if she now understood. Dr Rears appeared again at the doorway.

"Well, Summer, you shouldn't have walked into my house without permission." He sneered at me, once more his cocky self.

The haze reappeared, and I was unsure what to say at first. "Louise shouldn't be in your house," I blurted out and instantly regretted it. That wasn't my usual calm style of negotiation.

"No. She shouldn't be. And if you tell anyone, she will lose her leave," he warned, glancing over at Louise.

Louise's face dropped as he knew it would. "No, you can't tell anyone, Summer." Her eyes darted to me, full of panic and determination. I feared she would get angry with me if

I caused her to lose her leave. Or self-harm, which was far more likely. I had to play along if I wanted her onside.

"Of course I won't tell!" I looked her straight in the eye. My mouth hung open as if in shock that she thought I was capable of telling on her.

"See?" A grin spread across her face as she turned to Dr Rears. "She won't tell. Summer helps me. She's my friend. We're okay."

Annoyance flashed across Dr Rears' face. He knew damn well I would tell as soon as I had the chance. Joshua flashed through my mind again. I needed to get away from this psycho.

"Go downstairs, Louise," he commanded.

Louise faltered and looked at me. I smiled and nodded, not wanting her to be caught in any crossfire. She turned back and walked away, her steps echoing on the stairs. Before I knew it, Dr Rears was in front of me, his face right in mine. His breath was shallow and tickled my face along with the stench of cigarettes.

"You couldn't leave it alone, could you, you silly girl!"

"Leave what alone?" The growl that came out of my mouth surprised me. My fear had evaporated, and every fibre in my body was on fire. I wanted him to attack me. I wanted a reason to lay into the son of a bitch, to snap my head back and headbutt him straight in the nose, to see him suffer.

"Never mind, you will pay now," he spat nastily.

I laughed. "What are you going to do to me? You're going to let me go anyway, so I'll walk myself out now. My friend is waiting for me outside."

To my surprise, his face changed. He laughed too, a deep rumbling laugh.

"Me? I will do nothing! You still don't get it, do you? I

thought you were more clever than that, little Summer." He looked triumphant now, happy that he knew more than I did.

I squeezed my hand into a fist, digging my fingernails into my skin. It was taking all my energy not to lash out at him.

"No, it's not me! It's her!" he said.

"Who? Lucy?" I asked.

He laughed again. "For God's sake, child. Are you still bothered about Lucy? You're a mother, aren't you? A young boy?"

"Leave him out of this!" I roared in his face, spit landing on his nose. For the first time in my life, rage had overwhelmed me, and I was ready to kill.

"It's not what I would do! It's her, you stupid child! You need to think about your boy and leave this well alone. Do you understand?"

As much as I didn't want to admit it, his words brought me to my senses. What the hell was I doing about to pick a physical fight with a man twice my size and age?

"Fine!" I muttered. "I just want Joshua to be safe. Get out of my way and let me leave. I won't say anything."

He glared at me intently, his eyes inches away. My rage had subsided, but I glared back defiantly.

"You better," he finally whispered, "because if you don't, she will get your son too."

39

At Your Door...

Summer didn't see me sitting in my car as she made her way to *my* house. I couldn't believe the cheek of her, the stupid fucking ugly bitch. White-hot rage pierced my skin, the familiar burn taking over. I fought the urge to run after her. I'd tried to warn her to stay away the last time she'd visited. I'd driven the car right at her. The memory of her running down the street, her arms flailing all over, made me laugh out loud. The burning cooled. The laughter was like medicine.

She thought she'd disappeared by hiding in that old cow's driveway, but I knew where she was. I let her live. It wasn't time. Yet here she was again, attempting to ruin my plan. I watched her open the front door and considered following her. Lucy tried to do the same thing by taking Summer away from me. Rage induced, I'd allowed my feelings to overcome my need to hold on to the plan. I broke my own rules and showed myself to that awful woman to get help to stop Lucy. I'd had no choice. Thankfully, she hadn't recognised me. She was always too drunk to notice me.

I won, though. Lucy was where she belonged, and I knew she wouldn't mention me. She was too scared that I wasn't real, and her own mind was fucking with her. I'd helped her along with that. A lingering burning remained, but I pushed it away. I couldn't follow her. It wasn't time. I needed to get Joshua first. I needed to get him whilst I still knew where he was. If she moved him and I couldn't find him, then he would no longer be mine. Someone else would take him once she was dead, his grandma or maybe his dad. The burning grew again. It started deep within my chest. Joshua was mine. I couldn't bear the thought of someone else having him.

A thought occurred to me. If I took him, she would have to come to find him. And then I could kill her and keep Joshua easily. If they both disappeared, everyone would assume she took him away. Everyone would know how evil she was. But as I was about to drive off to get Joshua, Summer raced out the front door. Her steps were unsteady, and she kept looking behind her. *What the hell did he do now?* I grabbed my phone to call the blithering idiot doctor. I was going to have him for this. Him and that stupid patient he was fucking.

40

Summer

I stood for a moment, unable to move my frozen muscles. Mistrust made me slow. I couldn't tell if he was letting me leave or if it was some kind of trick. I forced my legs forward. It felt as though I was wading through thick mud. But he let me walk straight by him and out of the bedroom door. I stumbled downstairs, gripping the bannister, and searching for Louise, but I didn't see or hear her.

"I'm going now, Louise," I yelled but did not wait around for an answer. The urge to run was too strong.

I ran through the open front door and straight around the corner to jump into my car. My hands shook violently. I sat in the driver's seat cursing, wondering what to do about Louise, who I'd left behind with a supposed abuser. I started the engine first. There was no way I could think straight until I felt safe, and being able to make a quick getaway calmed me. I needed to help Louise, and I had to get back to Joshua, but I sat frozen in limbo. I was so sure coming here would give me answers, but instead I had more questions. I still needed to know who the hell *she* was. Then I remembered Mrs Timpson, and an idea formed in my mind. Not taking the time to think it through, I used my mobile to make a call and then got back out of the car. I half walked, half jogged to number 8, looking around me at all times. I didn't want Dr Rears or Louise to spot me still lurking around. Before I'd even reached her door, Mrs Timpson had opened it and stood beckoning me in.

"Hello, dear!" She seemed happy to see me.

"Hi!" I replied with a big smile to hide my agitation. "I was in the area, and I wanted to say thanks for the other day."

"Oh, no problem, love. Do you want to come in for a cup of tea? Oh, wait," she furrowed her brow, "a glass of water, maybe?"

"Ooh, yes, please." I feigned surprise that she'd ask me, despite knowing she would.

I once again walked into the living room, but this time I took a seat near the window amongst the plethora of clocks. Mrs Timpson took her time bringing the drinks. I assumed she was making a cup of tea for herself. All the while, I sat and stared at number 12. Nobody had left yet. I prayed they wouldn't. Not yet.

"Here you go, dear." Mrs Timpson returned with a glass of water for me. "Have you been feeling better?"

"Yes, thank you." I smiled and sipped my water, grateful my hands had stopped shaking. She eyed me suspiciously as if trying to decide whether I was indeed better. I must have still looked pale. "Better than I was, anyway." I tried to make my lie more believable. She nodded, sufficiently convinced.

"Horrible thing, anxiety. Our Betty used to suffer terribly."

She continued to tell me about Betty as if I knew who she was talking about. Despite the seriousness of the present situation across the road, I inwardly smiled. She was the perfect stereotype of a sweet, elderly lady. Though I didn't remember my own grandma, I'd always imagined her to be like this Mrs Timpson. I nodded and smiled for about ten minutes through her monologue about various people I'd never heard of, keeping one eye on the window at all times. I struggled to keep up with her, impatience pulling my attention away. Still, nothing happened at number 12.

The sharp noise of the house phone ringing made me jump. I laughed to make light of my nerves. Mrs Timpson threw me a sympathetic smile and patted my shoulder before picking up the house phone, explaining that she was waiting on her son to call. She wandered off into the kitchen to talk to the person on the line. It amazed me she had a phone modern enough to be wireless.

"Hello? Is that you, love? Speak up. You're talking too quietly," she said to who I assumed was her son as she walked away.

I stood up under the pretence of stretching my legs and turned my full attention to number 12 through the window, willing something to happen. And finally, it did. The noise was faint at first, and I strained my ears to make sure I hadn't imagined it. As the seconds passed, it gradually got louder. I noticed a car down the road pull away suddenly as if spooked by the noise. Eventually, the sirens were unmistakable, and two police cars came into view. They pulled up outside number 12. Two officers jumped out of each car, three men and one woman. I sat back down so they couldn't see me watching. One man approached the door and knocked loudly whilst another looked through the window. The woman and the other man stayed well away. Their heads were bent back, looking at the upper floor windows for any signs of movement.

I didn't recognise any of them from the previous day.

I'd expected to be nervous, but the electricity running through my veins was pure excitement. He was going to be caught, Louise was going to be safe, and so were Lucy and all the other patients.

Dr Rears answered in less than a minute. The officer who had been looking through the window joined his colleague to talk to Dr Rears, and the pair went inside with him. I had an itch to join them, to tell them what I knew, though I'd placed the call anonymously. I heard footsteps behind me. Mrs Timpson had returned from her phone call.

"Ooh, I thought I heard sirens. What's happening over there?" The drama immediately excited her.

"I'm not sure!" I lied, feigning the same interest she displayed. "Let's take a look, shall we?"

We both stood at the window. I didn't think anyone could see me, but I stayed back a bit. Fifteen minutes went past with Mrs Timpson concocting many potential scenarios. Maybe someone was hurt, maybe the doctor had been robbed, maybe he was involved with fraud. I marvelled at her creativity. I tried to ignore her for a moment as I noticed Louise leaving the house with one of the police officers. Her eyes were wide with fear. She slowly entered the back of one of the police cars, and after a couple of minutes, it drove off. I hoped they would take her straight back to the hospital and not the police station.

Five minutes later, Dr Rears left the property with the other officers. Annoyance flew through me as I saw he was not in handcuffs. *Surely he needed to be arrested straight away?* He climbed into the back of the police car by himself. I could imagine the charm offensive he was unleashing on the way to the station. I breathed a sigh of relief. Today did not go to plan, but I was one step closer to Joshua and I being safe. It was time for stage two.

41

Summer

It was afternoon by the time I left Coppice Court. The nerves stayed with me as I drove, and I made sure to keep an eye on all cars around me. I was positive I wasn't being followed. It was lunchtime and hunger cramps gripped my empty stomach. I visited the motorway services on the way home to order some food. The excitement of the morning had given me a tremendous appetite.

People milled in and out of the service station in a steady flow. Families dawdled inside chatting to each other, probably on their way to somewhere exciting. Business travellers ate alone or rushed around as if they were too important to smile or make room for other people. I didn't seem to fit in with any of them as I made my way to the fast-food outlet to order a burger and chips. I sat alone at a table in the corner with my back to the wall, where I could see all angles.

The burger and chips were delicious. I managed half of the meal before I couldn't wait any longer. I had to make the second call. The one I'd been putting off. I made my way back through the service station to the peace and quiet of my car. Once in the driver's seat, doors locked, I took out my phone and scrolled to the top of my contacts list to find Aaron's number. The phone kept ringing until it went to his voicemail. I rang again, but still no answer. I threw my phone to the side in annoyance. I'd expected him to be waiting for my call. I considered calling Swanson. He had said to call if I needed anything, I wanted to know what was happening with Dr Rears, what Lucy had told the police, and what Aaron had said. If I could get more information, I could figure out who had been following me. That was stage two of my plan. Swanson was probably too clever to let anything slip, but it was worth a try. I had nothing to lose by calling.

Butterflies took flight in my stomach as I found Swanson's card in my glove box and entered his number into the keypad. I paused before connecting the call, trying to figure out what to say to him, but nothing came to mind. Fuck it. I'd wing it. The phone rang long enough for me to consider hanging up before Swanson's deep voice finally answered.

"DI Swanson speaking."

Shit. Why did I think I'd wing it?

"Hi, DI Swanson." I used my best business voice to speak to him. The same sharp tone I sometimes used with hospital social workers or lawyers if they didn't give me what I needed to assist a patient. "It's Summer Thomas."

He paused before answering. I wondered what was going through his head. *Was he happy to hear from me?*

"How can I help, Miss Thomas?"

"I wanted to see if you had any further questions for me." The words came out without thinking. Thank God I'd actually found something to say.

"Yes, we do. I'm in the station right now if you'd like to come down?"

"Yes, okay." I could ask him about Aaron and Dr Rears while I was there. I could gauge his reaction better face to face. It's harder to say no to someone in person, though I doubted it would make a difference to the seasoned detective. We said our goodbyes before I pulled away from the service station and back onto the motorway. Twenty minutes later, I was walking into the cool reception area of the police station. I hadn't realised yesterday how modern it was, but I noticed it this time. The area had the smell of fresh paint. The walls were a cold blue colour, broken by random blocks of white. Fresh posters about crime rates and support groups dotted the walls, and a long counter took up the whole left side of the room. All the receptionists were behind thick safety glass.

I tentatively strolled up to one receptionist and told her I was there to see DI Swanson. She smiled at me and told me to take a seat to the right. She was the kind of jolly person who was instantly likable. Life must be much easier if you have that kind of ease around people. I'd probably be a better advocate if I was, and Joshua might still have a proper family. I was so lost in my thoughts that I was surprised when Swanson appeared before me after a minute or two. I briefly wondered if he was eager to see me. After saying an awkward hello, he led me into a room similar to the one we were in the previous day. I was glad to note that the rude DI Hart was nowhere to be seen.

"So, Miss Thomas, shall we continue our previous conversation?" Swanson asked.

"Call me Summer." I smiled. *Was I flirting?* I stopped smiling. "And before we do so, can I ask if Aaron is still in custody?"

"Without your full statement, we had little to charge him

with. So he was released yesterday with strict instructions not to contact you." He tried to smile reassuringly, but it looked more akin to a grimace.

"Right. And what did he tell you?" I asked.

"How about I ask some questions first, and then we'll go over what other people have said?"

I sighed, but nodded my agreement.

"So start from how you know Aaron, please."

"From work. Well, actually, I used to know him a few years ago when we were both at university. He was a friend of a friend. I didn't know him too well."

I stopped and studied the foreboding figure before me. His serious brown eyes stared down at his notepad. His large hand made the pen look tiny as he scribbled notes. He gave off the impression that he could protect anyone from anything. I tried to stick to the plan, to work alone and find out the truth. Yet, for some inexplicable reason, a powerful urge to tell him the truth overtook me. Before I knew it, I had told him much more than I'd planned. I told him everything I knew. All about Lucy, except for my dream. All about Aaron, except for the sex. I told him all I knew about Dr Rears, apart from my earlier visit, and that I believed Lucy when she accused him of abuse. Someone had helped her to escape, and it must have been someone on the inside. It had to be someone who wanted something from her in return for getting out. He raised his eyebrows at some parts but didn't interrupt me once. He allowed me to keep talking, and the more I talked, the harder it was to stop. It was like verbal diarrhoea.

"There's the other woman, too," I said tentatively after I'd finished discussing Dr Rears and his misdeeds. "I keep seeing her everywhere. I thought Lucy was following me, but she can't be now. She's back in the hospital, and I still saw the woman yesterday at the emergency room."

His head shot up at these words, and I looked away from his gaze. That was the part that concerned me the most, where he would accuse me of being crazy, of seeing things.

"Has anyone else seen this woman?" he asked his first question since the onslaught of my verbal diarrhoea.

"Aaron was with me once, outside a cafe near my flat, but he denied seeing her." I noticed his eyebrow raise. "But my mum has seen her," I added. "She went to my mum's house yesterday to tell her I had been taken. She must have seen it happen. So she must have been following me then, too." I remembered the bang at my flat door. Had that been her? Was she trying to scare me?

My face flushed as he continued to look at me. Tears stung the corner of my eyes, threatening to flow any second. I blinked them back. I hadn't confided in anyone for so long.

"I was scared she was after my son. He's six. I sent him to his dad's last night." I shrugged. "I don't know what she wants, but I don't think it's a friendly stalker. It's the way she looks at me. She could have been the person calling you, trying to make me look crazy."

"Okay," he said, "here's what I'm going to do. I'm going to interview Dr Rears and find out about this mystery woman. Then I'm going to call you and update you. Okay? I'm going to help make sure you're safe, Miss Thomas."

I smiled gratefully at him, though I was irked that he didn't call me Summer. My small smile wasn't enough to convey the appreciation I felt, but it was all I could manage. Exhaustion had hit me worse than the blow Lucy had given me yesterday. "What do I do now, though? Wait?" I asked.

"Yes." He replied in an authoritative manner which half made me want to argue with him. I had never been good with authority. "Go home, sit, and wait. My job is to help you, and that's what I'm going to do. No sneaking around by yourself, okay?"

I thanked him, and he walked me back to the reception area. Before walking away, he told me again to sit at home and wait for his call. I think he knew I would not listen. I would go home, but I would not sit and wait. This woman knew where I lived. Where Joshua lived, and I couldn't bear to be apart from him any longer.

I made a plan on the short drive back to my flat. I would make sure Mum knew to continue to stay with her sister, and I would collect some things for Joshua and me. I was already off work for the week, and he could pull a sickie from school. We would go to a hotel, but not the one down the road. We'd go away on a holiday, alone. The way we worked best. I planned for all the items we would need as I walked from the flat car park and through the front door of my building. We would need a phone charger, Joshua's tablet, some books, clothes—but my planning was cut short when I reached my flat and found my front door wide open. Someone was inside my flat.

42

Summer

The familiar anxiety prickled at my body. I slowly backed away, as if the door itself would attack me if it heard me moving. I reached the corridor door and yanked it open. My footsteps echoed loudly as I ran down the marble staircase and out into the fierce October wind. I didn't stop until I got to my car, jumped in and locked it. I started the engine, but I wasn't sure where to go. I grabbed my phone with shaking hands. It took me a few tries to unlock the screen with my thumbprint.

I had four missed calls from Aaron. Was it him in my flat? Trying to make sure I was okay? I hadn't spoken to him since the complete debacle with Lucy. Maybe he was worried enough to break in. I called him back, desperately hoping I was right despite the unlikeliness of it being true.

"Summer?" Aaron answered on the second ring.

"Yes, it's me. What the hell has been going on, Aaron?"

"Look, it got out of hand, okay. I didn't think she was going to hurt you! She's so paranoid. And I'm in a bit of a situation—"

"You are?! I've been knocked out, kidnapped, tied up, caught trespassing, and now someone's broken into my flat!"

"What?? Are you there now? Are you safe?"

"I didn't go inside. I'm out in the car park now. I was kind of hoping it was you. If not, I'm going to call the police."

"What? Why would I break into your flat?"

"I don't know what you're capable of after yesterday."

"She hit me too, Summer. Knocked me clean out, and when I woke, she'd tied you up. I'd never hurt you. Look, don't call the police. I won't be able to come help then, they've told me to stay away from you, but I need to see you. I need to tell you some things."

"Oh, I wonder why they've said to stay away from me?" I rolled my eyes, even though he couldn't see me.

"Okay. I deserved that. Now sit in your car and be ready to drive off if you see her. She's dangerous."

"If I see who?" I demanded, sick of not being told the full story.

"I'll be there in five minutes." He hung up. I cursed him loudly, despite being alone.

I sat in my car, waiting and looking for any signs of the mystery figure. Whoever she was, she scared grown men half to death. It was nearing dinner time, and the sky was changing to a dark blue. It was going to be a night sky soon, and I prayed for Aaron to hurry. I did not want to be sneaking around in the dark. I wanted to get our things, get Joshua, and get the hell away from Derby while Swanson did his job. True to his word, I spotted a tall figure darting towards the car park after a few minutes. I waited until he was a hundred feet away before getting out of my car to greet him.

"Hi," he said breathlessly as he reached me, his face blotchy and sweaty.

"Hi." I was curt with him, still angry from the danger he had put me in the day before.

"Look, give me your keys and stay in your car. I'll check it out for you," he said after a few seconds of trying to get his breath back.

"No! I'm coming with you." I knew I was being stubborn. A part of me would have preferred to pass him the keys and stay away, but I was already embarrassed that I wanted his help. I couldn't take any further rescuing or indebtedness.

He motioned for me to get behind him, and we carefully walked to the front door. I passed him my keys and he let us in. There was no one in the grand entry hall. The chandelier loomed over us as we made our way up the staircase once again. Friday night's antics with Aaron came back to me as we walked, and I felt a pang of regret for the first time. We entered my corridor and made our way slowly to the flat door. It was closed. I looked up at Aaron, wondering if he was going to accuse me of making it up.

"It was wide open, I swear." I whispered, despite no one being around us. He nodded and put his finger to his lips.

I pointed at the right key for him to use, and he unlocked the door as slowly as he could. It was impressive how silently he managed it. I grappled with my urge to grab the keys from him and throw open the door. Still silent, he manoeuvred the handle down to open the door. It didn't squeak, but it rubbed noisily against the thick carpet. We stood looking in, listening to the silence. Nothing moved. Nobody jumped out at us. It looked completely normal. Aaron moved forwards to the entry hall and stood still to listen again. Still silent. I followed him into the hall. *Had I been seeing things? Was the door even open when I got back?*

As soon as we reached the lounge, my fears of hallucinations were silenced. My laptop lay on the floor, the screen smashed. Someone had thrown papers and books all over the room. They had taken pictures of Joshua and me from the wall and thrown them on the floor, shattered and unrecognisable.

At first glance, it looked like nothing had survived. The TV was cracked. The coffee table overturned. Tears stung my eyes, and I let them come. I didn't care if Aaron saw. I looked around for Joshua's things, wondering how I was going to afford to replace his tablet and all of his toys.

A small wave of relief washed over me as I remembered his tablet was with him. He'd brought it to Mum's and then to Richard's. That was the most expensive *toy* he had and his favourite item. Everything else I'd have to replace bit by bit. As I looked around to find his broken toys, I realised none of his toys or books had been thrown on the floor, but neither were they in the place they usually were. Panic gripped my stomach as if someone had punched it.

"We need to talk," Aaron said. I'd actually forgotten about him.

"Where the fuck are Joshua's things?!" I shouted at him. I didn't care at all about what he had to tell me. I cared about one thing.

"What?" Aaron looked at me with a confused expression.

"Joshua's toys, his books, they're not smashed on the floor. Where the fuck are they?"

His face changed as he realised the implications of what I was saying. I grabbed my phone out of my jeans pocket. My entire body was shaking, but I refused to lose my calm completely. I could not fail Joshua. I got Richard's number up and pressed dial.

"Hey, Summer. You on your way?" Richard's easygoing voice made me want to reach down the phone and slap him.

"Richard, is Joshua okay?" I yelled down the phone.

"What? Yes, he's fine. Why wouldn't he be?" He took a defensive tone.

"Look, can you see him right now? Is he with you?"

"Yes, he's eating his dinner." He sounded confused. "What's going on? Are you okay?"

"I think so, but someone has broken into the flat."

"Oh shit, have they taken anything?"

"Yes, Joshua's things. They've smashed all my stuff up."

Richard was silent then as he tried to take in what I was saying. "Why would they take a child's things?" he asked eventually, caution in his voice.

"I don't know for sure, but I feel like we need to go away, Richard, for a few nights on a little holiday. You don't mind, do you? I've told the police. They will catch whoever this is, and then we can come home."

"He could stay here," Richard suggested.

"He could, but I think he'd be happier on a holiday. It would be exciting for him. He won't know anything is wrong." I didn't say it out loud, but Joshua hated being away from me for more than a night or two, and he'd already been away since Friday. It would devastate him if I didn't spend tonight with him.

"Yeah, okay," Richard agreed. "I won't tell him yet. When do you think you'll be over?"

"Well, I need to speak to the police, so it might be an hour or two," I said. "Can you look at last-minute hotels and B&Bs for us, please? Anywhere child-friendly. Maybe near a theme park or something, someplace far away."

SUMMER

"Okay, that's fine. Keep me updated." He hung up the phone.

"Summer, we need to talk." Aaron tried again to get my attention. I was ready now that I knew Joshua was safe.

"Yeah, we do," I spat angrily at him. "My child is in danger and no one will even tell me who from! Who the fuck is this mystery woman all of you grown-ass men are so scared of? Because I'm telling you now, if I get my hands on her, I will go down for fucking murder."

I shook with the same rage that had come close to winning me over at Dr Rears' house. I needed someone to blame for this mess, and Aaron was right in the firing line.

"Sit," Aaron ordered. "Let's talk."

"Tell me what to do one more time, Aaron, and I swear to God you will regret it. You fucking sit and tell me what's happening." I knew I sounded petulant, but I couldn't help it. The rage was winning. My instinct to protect Joshua was trumping any kind of fear or anxiety.

Aaron stood still. "Is Joshua at Richard's?" he asked.

I nodded. "Now answer my fucking question, Aaron. Who the hell is doing this?"

"Wait, we need to get somewhere safe. She could be back any minute."

"Who though, Aaron? You're not talking about Lucy, are you?" I waved my hands in the air. Aaron shook his head. "Then who? For fuck's sake, tell me who is doing this?"

For the first time that evening, I stood still and looked at Aaron. I noticed the fear in his eyes. Whoever this was had him spooked big time, like with Dr Rears. I knew I should be scared, too. I needed to calm down before I did something stupid, but every instinct I had was pushing me to defend Joshua. Before having a child, I never thought I could hurt anybody. But I'd known as soon as Joshua was born, I'd kill for him. I don't even think I'd even feel guilty.

Aaron appeared to be considering what to tell me, and I tried to reach the placid, gentle, collected me. The normal me. But anger had consumed that version of me with a rage born of maternal instinct. I was more dangerous than the average psychopathic murderer. Then, someone else appeared who I could aim that rage at, the same someone that scared all of these grown men. Someone who had never left the flat.

43

Summer

The figure stood in the doorway, blocking any exit from the lounge. Her black hair was scraped back into a ponytail. She wore dark trousers and a dark jumper. A large kitchen knife glinted in her hand. This was the same woman that had knocked on my mum's door and the one who had been following me. The monster that was a danger to Joshua. For once, she didn't hide or run away. She stood silently, her entire focus on me. A slow grin spread across her face, showing her yellow teeth. Her skin was patchy, not burnt like Lucy's, but she looked like a patchwork doll who had been stitched together with different fabrics. From afar, the two women certainly looked similar. It was seeing the skin close up that finally enabled me to recognise her. A gasp escaped me as I pieced together bits of what had been happening over the last few days.

"You?" It was all I could say at first. The woman before me laughed in such a deep voice it sounded like a growl.

"Yes, dumbass, it's me. Didn't even recognise me, did you? Walking around the ward, telling us all what to do, and being besties with the patients. Do you recognise me now, Summer?"

I nodded and felt my resolve harden. The shock had allowed my rage to subside. I was calmer, and I could think straight. If I could think of a plan, then I could get out of this without being hurt and without hurting anyone else. I recognised Emma now, the lead nurse from Bluebell Ward. The same Emma who had been off sick yesterday afternoon. In all my time on the ward, she had never looked me in the eye. She was always monitoring the patients, too busy to talk to me, or so I had thought. All that time, she had been keeping her distance so that I wouldn't recognise her. Her name wasn't Emma at all. She didn't even have blonde hair. It must have been an excellent wig.

"You...look well." I couldn't think of anything else to say. She had lost a lot of weight since I had last seen her, well before she became Emma. My response once again set off her deep laugh.

"Not that I need you to tell me, but yes, I look good. Your brother helped me along." She grinned again.

"What is going on, Marinda? Have you hurt somebody?" Using her actual name was a gamble. I was unsure if it would provoke or calm her. It didn't seem to do either.

"You have no clue what's going on, do you?" She rolled her eyes as if I was an idiot. "It's not me who hurts them. It's the good Dr Rears!" she said as if this was obvious to anyone with half a brain.

"Dr Rears let me go. He said it's you I have to watch. You're the dangerous one," I said with a shrug.

She lost her smile, her eyes flashing with anger. I'd never seen her like this. Marinda was always the calm one. She helped my brother as much as she could. They'd been together for an entire year before he attacked my mother. She was training to be a make-up artist so she could support them both after he lost his job. She used her make-up well on the ward. I hadn't had any inkling it was her.

"I'm not the one who hit you." She shrugged. "I went to get help."

"Why did you get help if you're so angry with me?"

"So I can hurt you now." She laughed. "I've been watching you and Joshua. I came here to get him. But he isn't here. Where is he?" She smiled again, knowing her words would rile me.

She was right, but I *knew* Marinda. Or at least I used to know her. I remembered watching her and my mum talk and laugh. Before Dad's death, Mum would help her with her skin in the summer when her pityriasis versicolor flared up around her left eye and cheek. A flaky skin condition that also caused discolouration. It was made worse by humid summer temperatures and Marinda had hyperhidrosis. After Dad died, she would take me to the shop and buy me sweets when Mum was comatose on the sofa. She looked after me the night Eddie lost his battle with the devil. I'd even tried looking for her once, whilst searching for Eddie. I couldn't fathom why she would hate me.

"Why are you following me, Marinda?"

"Payback time." She cocked her head to the side and watched my reaction, still grinning at me.

"Payback for what?"

"For what?" She mocked my voice in a whiny tone. "You know what. You're the reason Eddie went away, and I was left alone. Your statement put him in the hospital. Don't play mock innocent with me. You feel so guilty that you haven't even visited him once. You haven't even apologised to him! And all this time, he's been in that awful place, drugged up to the eyeballs for no reason. I've hated you ever since you opened your big fat mouth to the police. And then you walked on to the ward a few months ago like nothing had ever happened. Imagine my horror when I found out that while he is trapped in there, you've been swanning about pretending to care about patients! Thinking you're clever with your degrees and your supposed awards. I can see lies, remember? You are a *liar*."

Of course, Mum always thought Marinda had her own mental health issues because she could see colours when people spoke. Synesthesia is not a mental health concern, but Marinda interpreted these colours as truth or lies, good or evil. I remembered her telling me after Eddie had been taken away that his aura had changed to an evil colour since she met him. Red or black, I couldn't remember, but it had terrified me. I noticed Aaron moving slowly from the corner of the room. He was watching Marinda. She was completely focused on me. I couldn't tell if she knew he was in the room or not. She had surely seen him when she entered. I didn't look at him, keeping my gaze on Marinda.

"I didn't know where he was," I told her. I didn't feel guilty about what I'd done. I was a child. Eddie was ill, and he'd needed help. Something else she'd said had caught my attention, though. "What do you mean, drugged up for no reason? Eddie was severely ill."

She rolled her eyes. "What do you even know about Eddie's so-called illness?"

"Not much. He heard voices a lot. He saw the devil telling him to hurt people. Telling him to hurt Mum. I assumed he was a paranoid schizophrenic."

"Your mum was a pain in the neck, Summer. She was always pissed on vodka or gin. She even had the cheek to call *me* nuts once because of my gift! She tried to get Eddie to break up with me! But I saw through her. She was a waste of space. I wanted her gone *and* I wanted the house. It would have been my first, proper home." She waved her hands as she spoke.

"What do you mean?"

"The house would have gone to Eddie." She smirked at me.

"So what?"

"Soo… Eddie was mine. The house would have been mine. He didn't hear fucking voices. I needed him to see what your Mum was really like. She was the one who needed to go, not me."

"I don't understand?" My fight was leaving me as the repercussions of her words hit me. "He didn't hear voices. He lied? Is that what you mean?"

She shook her head slowly, a smirk still lined her face. "The only voice Eddie heard was mine."

"Bullshit," I snapped. "And if it is true, then you need to be in the fucking hospital."

"I'm not ill, Summer. I'm in charge of an entire ward of fucking nut jobs. How did I get there if I'm so ill? Your mum started it all. Plus I had fun pushing Eddie and seeing how far I could take it. It wasn't too hard, to be fair, thanks to Daddy dying. I wanted to see how far I could push him, and I wanted that house all to myself. I wanted Eddie all to myself. I would have stopped once your interfering bitch of a mother was out of our lives. And I nearly did it too. If it wasn't for you hiding under that fucking table and snitching up your own brother. You ruined it for me, Summer. I could have had that house, with Eddie doing everything I needed, maybe even our own family. My *first* proper family. But now your boy will have to do."

Her words made me feel sick. I couldn't listen to her anymore. I needed to change the subject and keep her distracted so that Aaron could get to her.

"How did you get in here?" I tried talking about the physical acts she had accomplished to stop her from talking about my family.

"I've been in here a few times." She smirked. I bent over and heaved, unable to hold it in anymore. "I took your keys from your locker, had it copied in twenty minutes at a shop down the road."

"Have you been in here at night?" I remembered my dream.

"Yes." She smirked again. "I watched you as you slept. Then you suddenly screamed and jumped up like a fucking lunatic. I shut the door and ran off."

"What happened to Lucy? Did you help her escape?" I changed the subject again while I tried to regain some composure and ignore the bile in my throat.

"Oh, for God's sake, you always needed to know every little detail, didn't you? Yes, I took Lucy off the ward to be a good girl for Dr Rears. She wasn't supposed to fucking run off. I also told her that you'd said you didn't want to see her." She laughed.

"A good girl for Dr Rears?" I didn't want to know any more, but I had to keep her talking as Aaron inched his way over to her.

"Yes. Those stupid girls at the hospital are worthless," she spat. "I have my fun and then let them go. It's not like I've killed anybody."

"Your fun?"

"I just scare them a bit. They'll do anything for me. For their leave or to get out of that fucking hell hole of a hospital. Once we're at the house, they do what they're told. Or should do. Lucy was an idiot. She was supposed to clean up, and then she could have gone shopping. I never saw her again."

My brain was faltering from trying to process what Marinda was telling me. I couldn't focus. Nothing made sense.

"Jesus, Marinda. What do you mean, they do as they're told? What do you tell them to do?"

She smiled and leaned towards me. "Whatever the fuck I want from them." She emphasised each word as if she got a kick from it. "Aww, do you think I'm bad? You should see what I caught Rears doing last year! It was he who gave me the idea. He made me realise they would do whatever we wanted. I don't shout at them or beat them. They behave, and they continue to get leave. It's simple, really. They've all been through far worse!"

"What did you catch him doing?"

"Fucking!" She laughed again. "Fucking! Can you believe it? I knew he wasn't right, like you. I followed him all the way out to some field with Aaliyah. She was barely sixteen. I lost them down some country road and the next minute found them fucking. He had her bent over the bonnet, his lily-white arse sticking out!"

"So, instead of reporting him, you help him?" My stomach churned again.

"God, no. He begged and begged me not to say anything. He said he loved her, for fuck's sake. Pathetic. How could anyone love that? Anyway, that's when I realised we could work together. We could cover each other's backs. I had no interest in helping him. I wanted to see what the patients would do for leave. I don't have sex with them like he does. I'm not like that pervert."

"You don't sound much better." The words were out of my mouth before I could stop them.

"They look after me in other ways because I look after them. There's nothing wrong with it." She looked at me defiantly, clearly believing her own bullshit. "Everyone was pleased. Well, until you turned up and Lucy ran away. She wasn't even supposed to be on leave. I couldn't very well say she'd run out of the locked hospital, could I now? I couldn't admit I'd taken her out, regardless. What was I supposed to do?" She shrugged her shoulders.

"Why not call the police?"

"So Lucy could talk to them? If I lost Dr Rears, who would I have to help? The idiot is terrified that I will tell someone what I saw, what I know. He does everything I need, and I'd rather the police didn't take that away from me. Then you had to stick your nose in like you did with Eddie and that sold it. *You* have to go."

"You'd never have gotten away with it even if it wasn't for me. What about the other staff? Other patients?"

"The patients were easy enough to keep quiet. Tell them they were hallucinating the dead ghost of Lucy. They soon asked for more meds and shut the fuck up. Staff were harder, but luckily most are bank staff anyway, and I know how to keep the ones that aren't quiet. Don't I, Aaron?" She turned to look at Aaron, and alarm crossed her face.

Everything that happened next was a complete blur. Aaron ran towards her in an attempt to tackle her. Something shiny and silver flashed before I'd even moved to help him.

"No!" I screamed, but it was too late. The blade slid into

Aaron's body. He looked winded and fell to the floor, gasping for breath.

"You next, bitch." Marinda barely flinched as she removed her knife from Aaron's gut. She rushed towards me. I turned to run, but she was coming from the only doorway. I was trapped.

44

Summer

"Summer?" A nervous call came from the hallway. I knew that voice.

"Kelly, run!" I yelled as loudly as I could, running to the other side of the lounge to get Marinda to follow me.

If she followed me away from the door, then I could make a run for it and get Aaron some help. Horror flooded me as Marinda turned and ran out into the corridor. She was heading straight for Kelly. I ran after her as fast as my legs would allow, yelling over and over for Kelly to run, dreading what I was about to find. Immense relief flooded me to see Kelly standing in the corridor alone, though she was white as a ghost.

"What the fuck, Summer? Who's the crazy bitch?" Kelly's mouth was wide open as she stared at me.

"Where is she?" I demanded.

"She ran out the door." Kelly shrugged and pointed over her shoulder.

"Look, I haven't got time to explain, but lock the door and call an ambulance." She still stared at me in confusion. "Kelly, now! Aaron's been stabbed," I said breathlessly.

I made sure she was moving to lock the door before I ran back to check on Aaron. He lay on his left side, gasping in short, quick breaths. Blood leaked from his shirt and covered his hands. I knelt next to him and took off my cardigan to bind the wound. My first aid training brimmed in my mind, recovery position, hold the wound, stop the bleeding. Aaron looked up at me, eyes wide with terror. He made a gurgling sound as he tried to form words.

"Shh, it will be okay." I tried to soothe him. "She's gone. The door is locked. We're safe. An ambulance is on its way. It will be here any minute."

"No," he mumbled, "my mum…Mum…"

I ached to hear him calling for his mum. His eyes closed.

"Aaron!" I said sharply. His eyes flickered back open to look at me. Kelly was next to me now, but I barely heard what she was saying. "You need to stay awake for me. Can you do that, Aaron? Can you stay awake for me? Your mum's on her way." I lied. "Stay with me, Aaron,"

I kept talking the whole time, rambling about going for a drink soon. About stupid memories of us as students. Anything to keep him awake. Kelly had gone outside to wait for the ambulance. She finally returned with two male paramedics five minutes later. Thank God they were so fast. By then, Aaron's skin reminded me of the wax models in London's museum, and his eyes had rolled to the back of his head.

"Hi, Aaron, I'm Ben. I'm going to help you, okay? I'm going to cut your top so I can reach the wound, then I'm going to give you some pain relief. Try to stay awake for us, Aaron." They talked constantly. I could finally step back and let them take over.

They got to work straight away, trying to give him gas and air, but he wasn't able to breathe it in. They injected something, but I couldn't tell if it was to clean the wound or give him pain relief. I didn't know how they could be so calm. They sealed the wound with all sorts of bandages and kept up a one-sided conversation with him while they worked.

I stood beside them, feeling helpless. Then I remembered Marinda. Where the hell had she run off to? *Was she looking for Joshua?* He'd be waiting for me at Richard's. Richard would think it was me knocking on the door, like I had the other day. I stepped into the kitchen and grabbed my phone to call Richard. He answered abruptly.

"Hey. Look, something has happened." I wasn't sure how to tell him.

"What now?" He didn't sound angry, more surprised.

"Well, it turned out the patient who hit me yesterday was running from someone else. It is the same someone who turned up at my flat today and smashed the stuff. I'm okay, but she's dangerous. I wanted to make sure she doesn't know where Joshua is. You haven't seen anyone, right?"

"No, nothing. Look, don't worry about Joshua. He's fine with me, and my brother is here, too. Make sure you're safe and then call me. Maybe stay at your mum's?"

Shit. My mum. I couldn't be sure if she was still at her sister's or back at home. Marinda knew where my mum lived. She hadn't moved house in thirty years. I didn't know if Marinda blamed Mum, too, but at least she hadn't hurt Mum or Joshua when she had the chance yesterday.

"Okay, I have to go." I hung up on Richard and dialled Mum's number. No answer. I called again and again, but she didn't pick up.

I felt eyes on me and looked up. Kelly was standing in the doorway, watching me. She was still paler than I'd ever seen her. "Who are you calling?" she asked.

"My mum. That crazy bitch knows where she lives. She isn't answering."

"Try calling your Aunt?" She suggested.

"I don't have her number saved." I tried one more time before pushing past Kelly to check on Aaron.

The paramedics were putting Aaron onto a stretcher. I couldn't believe he'd risked his life for me. "I'll see you at the hospital," I promised as they carried him away.

I looked back at Kelly. I'm going to my mum's. I need to make sure she's safe."

"I'm coming too. You can tell me what the fuck is going on while I drive." She took my keys out of my hand.

"Kelly, she's crazy! Stay here and tell the police where I've gone. They'll be here any minute."

"No fucking way. I'm coming too." She walked past me and waited for me in the communal hallway. I was secretly glad she was so stubborn.

We walked out together, side by side, but as she drove off, my heart sank. Maybe if I had opened up to someone else in the first place, Aaron wouldn't be on a hospital stretcher fighting for his life. Maybe this was all my fault. I prayed that Mum would be okay.

45

Summer

I called Mum's mobile multiple times on the drive over to her house, but there was still no answer. I was furious with her.

"Call the police. They'll be on their way to yours. We might as well tell them where we think she might be," Kelly said.

"Actually, I know who I can call." I checked the numbers I had called earlier that day and found the unsaved number that I knew must be Swanson's.

"DI Swanson." He finally answered after letting it ring.

"Hi, it's Summer Thomas. Look, I need help. That stalker has just stabbed Aaron, and I think I know where she's going next." I was far more blunt than usual, but my mind was racing. I'd never considered a life without Mum before. Joshua would be devastated. I had to make sure she was safe.

"Where?" was all he said. I gave him my mum's address.

"Don't go there. We will check on her for you. You go somewhere safe." He hung up before I had time to tell him I was nearly there.

Kelly glanced at me. "I'm still going," I said. She nodded.

It usually took twenty minutes to get to Mum's house. Kelly did it in twelve minutes flat. As we drove up to Mum's house, I looked for any sign that she was home. There was a lamp in the lounge window, but she always left that on in the evenings. Although it was dark by then and difficult to see, I searched the shadows for Marinda and told Kelly to park past the house in an attempt not to alert Marinda if she was inside. We got out and closed the car doors as quietly as we could before jogging quickly back to Mum's. There was nothing to hide behind on the drive as we approached the house. We were out in the open and needed to be quick. I looked through the bottom corner of the living room window, bent down, trying to make sure I couldn't easily be spotted if anyone was in there. I saw a shadow in the far corner, but I couldn't tell who it was without standing to look. I rang Mum's phone one more time and heard the ringtone blasting out from inside the living room, but the shadowy figure ignored it. I couldn't hear any voices. Maybe Mum was in there alone. Maybe Marinda had already killed her. My heart skipped a beat.

I looked at Kelly and nodded my head towards the front door, gradually pulling the handle down.

"Stop." The loud command came from behind us. I nearly jumped out of my skin. I felt Kelly startle too. A frightened look passed between us as we turned around simultaneously.

Swanson and Hart stood at the end of the drive. They made a strange pair standing side by side with such a size difference. Hart was even shorter than me.

"Are you going inside?" I ignored Hart and looked at Swanson instead. My hand stayed on the handle.

"We're going to wait for the armed response unit. They'll be here soon," Swanson reassured me in his smooth, calm voice.

Soon? I didn't feel reassured.

"Don't open that door, Miss Thomas!" Hart insisted. She could clearly see me considering my options, but I was sick of talking.

I opened the door and ran inside. The detectives had ruined the element of surprise, so there was no point in sneaking around anymore. I ran straight into the living room with Kelly quick on my heels, loyal to the end. I spotted my mum first. She sat at the far end of the dining table. It had been her shadow I could see from the window. She was sitting at the table eating fish and chips from a cardboard box as if nothing was happening. As if I hadn't just been threatened in my own home and a crazy person hadn't stabbed Aaron for protecting me. My worry turned to the usual resentment. She was never there for me when I needed her, not since Dad had died. She stood as I ran in, almost choking on a chip in the process.

"What the hell, Summer?" she shouted as she got over her coughing fit. "You scared me half to death. What's wrong?"

I ignored her because I had spotted the second person in the room. My mum hadn't touched a man since my dad had died. Yet sitting next to her was a man sharing her fish and chips. Dr Rears.

46

Summer

Dr Rears once again looked as shocked to see me as I was to see him. "You know each other?" he asked incredulously.

"Oh, this is Summer, my daughter," Mum said, "and her friend Kelly. Hi, Kelly dear."

"Hi," Kelly said, looking confused.

"Mum, what are you doing with Dr Rears?" I asked.

"Oh, do you two know each other? Well, we met last week on the bus." She smiled at him as I threw him a dark look. "We had lunch together yesterday, and we were supposed to go for a walk today. But Albert got held up, so fish and chip supper it was instead."

"Albert?" It took me a moment to realise that must be Dr Rears' first name. "Held up? He got arrested today for bringing vulnerable patients to his home and fucking them!" I spat. Mum's face dropped, and guilt grasped me. I could have worded it better. I hadn't noticed the detectives entering the room behind me. The sudden voice of Swanson made me jump yet again. He moved quietly.

"Mrs Thomas, I'm DI Swanson, and this is my colleague DI Hart."

Hart gave a strange, brief wave in my mum's direction before turning away. She was looking around the room, taking in every nook and cranny. I fought the urge to tell her to get out.

Swanson continued. "Has anyone been here today to threaten you?" He looked at me. "A woman, I believe?"

Mum looked even more confused now. Her day was getting stranger and stranger. "No. I only got home a couple of minutes ago. I was telling my daughter that my friend, this gentleman here, and I were supposed to go for a walk, but then we got fish and chips instead." She pointed towards the half-eaten food in front of her.

"So there's no one else in the house?" Swanson asked. "Can we look around to check? To make sure you're safe?"

"Yes, go ahead, but you won't find anyone," Mum waved towards the direction of the hall.

Swanson walked past us and set off to check the rest of the house, starting with the kitchen. Hart stayed behind but went to the window to look outside.

I turned back to Dr Rears. "Why are you with my mum? Did Marinda put you up to this?"

"Who is Marinda?" Dr Rears' brow furrowed as he looked at me.

"Marinda?" Mum asked. "Marinda Tanda?"

"Yes, Mum, I'll explain soon." Mum's mouth gaped open, and I turned my attention back to Dr Rears. "You know her as Emma Fahy. Her proper name is Marinda Tanda."

Dr Rears shifted uncomfortably in his seat. "I don't know what you're talking about," he said.

"So you happened to bump into *my* mum last week and hit

it off?" I rolled my eyes.

"Yes, as it happens, I did." He stood up. "Well, I'm going to get going. I have a prior engagement."

"You're not going anywhere. Sit down," Hart commanded. Dr Rears did as he was told without a word.

"Summer, Marinda Tanda is dangerous," Mum looked over at me.

"Yes, Mum. I know that now. She tried to kill me!" I threw my hands in the air in exasperation. "Wait, how do you know she's dangerous?"

"She egged Eddie on the night his demons got too much," Mum looked away. "She told him to make sure he did what the devil said or you would die too. She made him so much worse.."

"Jesus, Mum. You never told me that. She looked after me that night at the police station. She told me not to tell the police anything."

"I didn't know, Summer. I was unconscious. I made sure you were safe as soon as I woke up."

I looked away and didn't respond. There were too many eyes in the room listening to us. We could talk when everyone had left. At least I finally knew why Mum hadn't wanted me to look for Marinda or Eddie.

"Ms Thomas?" Hart directed her attention towards me. "If the woman isn't here, then where is she? We need to make finding her a priority if she's dangerous and armed."

"I don't know." I willed my brain to think harder. Then it came to me. "He knows." I pointed towards Dr Rears.

"I do not!" he protested.

"Sir, if you know where this lady might be, and you aren't

telling us, you could be in serious trouble. Especially if she hurts someone."

Dr Rears fell quiet for a moment. He appeared to be weighing up his options.

"Don't you think you're in enough trouble as it is?" she asked him.

He sighed sadly as if he was giving up. "Try 12 Coppice Court, Edwinstowe." He put his head in his hands.

Sirens wailed outside as two police cars pulled up. Hart got on the radio as Swanson returned from checking the house. He shook his head at her. He had found nothing.

"Redirect ARU to Coppice Court, Edwinstowe," she said into the radio. "You," she pointed at Dr Rears, "are coming to the station for more questioning. You clearly didn't tell us everything today, did you?"

He nodded weakly and stood to follow them out the front door. He avoided my mum's gaze as he left with the detectives. All three of them went outside to speak to the officers on the drive. I walked over to the window to watch them. One of the officers helped Dr Rears into the back of the car and climbed into the front seat. Another officer followed a minute later into the front passenger seat before they drove off.

The other two officers approached the house as the detectives walked to their own car. I saw Swanson climb into the driver's side of a dark Audi. I turned away from the window as the front door slammed shut behind the officers. I recognised one as PC Townsend. He had a different partner today who introduced herself as PC Middleton.

"We would like to ask you all a few questions." PC Townsend smiled around at us. "Starting with you, Miss Thomas. If that's okay?"

47

Swanson

Hart and Swanson arrived in Edwinstowe thirty minutes later, with their siren blaring through the cold evening air.

"Turn that noise off," Hart instructed as they approached Coppice Court. She took out her radio to check how close ARU was. Five minutes.

The Coppice was as quiet as they pulled up to number 12. Someone had abandoned a FIAT Punto on the drive and left the driver's door wide open. Hart checked to ensure the car was empty, whilst Swanson crept up to the front window, straining to see through the murky nets. He walked over to the front door and tried the handle. It was unlocked. The door creaked as it opened and the smell hit him as soon as he opened the door—dirt, rotten food, dust. He turned on his torch to check it out and noted bags of rubbish lining the kitchen at the far end of the property. A shiver ran down his spine. There was something not right about this house.

He could see the stairs and a door to his left. Careful to remain silent, he crept inside with Hart hot on his heels. He checked the door and found the living room. Empty. He continued to the stairs, the quiet feeling oppressive. Hart moved past him to check the kitchen. She came back seconds later and nodded. They ascended the stairs together, Swanson going first, straining to hear any signs of movement. The pair were silent as they moved in and out of each upstairs room. In the last bedroom, they looked at each other in frustration. The house was clear. Marinda was nowhere to be found.

"Any other ideas?" Hart asked.

Swanson walked over to the window of the bedroom, stroking his beard. He studied the street below.

"Tell ARU they may as well park close by," he said. "With that car on the front, she must be around somewhere."

Hart walked out of the room, barking orders into her radio. Swanson continued to stare out of the window, his mind working through the puzzle. He spotted a lone figure on the driveway of another property, not too far down the road. The figure was female and wore a baseball cap, which struck him as strange in the grey winter evening. She looked around as if searching for someone and then hurried away. She was walking away from number 8 Coppice Court.

Swanson kicked into gear and yelled for Hart as he ran down the stairs. She appeared in seconds.

"Where are ARU?" he demanded.

"Parked outside," she yelled after him as they reached the bottom corridor.

"Tell them down the street. The woman coming from number 8."

Hart did as he asked without question, using her radio to reach the ARU. As the pair approached the front door, they saw ARU jump out of their dark van parked across the street.

The woman noticed them too and broke out into a run. The ARU shouted for her to stop, but she ignored them. She was fast but no match for ARU or the detectives. Two of the ARU officers reached her first and tackled her to the ground. She screamed and kicked out like a wild boar, but they were far bigger than her. She was handcuffed within a few seconds. The ARU officers dragged her over to where Swanson was bent over, close to number 12, gasping for air. He wasn't built for speed. The woman no longer appeared to have a weapon, but she did have blood spattered on the front of her top. She was breathing heavily, and tears streamed down her face.

"Marinda Tanda?" Swanson asked.

"My name is Emma Fahy. I have no idea who Marinda Tanda is, but you've got the wrong woman!" she spat at him through anguished tears. Her eyes looked all around as if trying to plan an escape route.

"Care to explain the blood on your top?" Hart asked her.

The woman didn't answer. Instead, she stopped sobbing and focussed her gaze on Swanson. Her eyes were wild, and spit foamed at her mouth. Swanson instinctively took a step back. Getting spat on wasn't fun.

"What were you doing in number 8?" he asked her. Questioning would usually be reserved for the police station, but he needed to know if she had an accomplice or if she'd hurt someone.

"I wasn't in there," the woman answered far too quickly. "I heard a shout and knocked at the door, but nobody answered."

Hart shared a look with Swanson. "Take her to the station," Hart commanded the ARU officer. The woman started shouting and kicking again as the officer dragged her away.

Swanson hurried towards number 8 Coppice Court, with

Hart once again following closely behind him. He made his way up the cobbled driveway and past the grey car parked there, checking inside the vehicle as he passed. It looked as though it hadn't been driven in a long time. He reached the door and knocked loudly three times, waiting for a response. Hart peered through the front window for a moment.

"Inside now!" She yelled.

Swanson kicked open the front door with one large boot and ran inside with Hart right behind him. He ran up the short corridor and burst into the living room, familiar adrenaline pumping. It didn't take him long to see why Hart had yelled for them to go inside. On the floor, right in front of the window, lay an elderly lady, her clothes soaked with blood. Swanson knelt next to her and checked for a pulse. Silently, he looked up at Hart and shook his head.

48

Summer

I put the phone down, tears stinging my eyes. It made no sense. Why the hell would Marinda hurt Mrs Timpson? Did Marinda know she'd helped me? Mrs Timpson didn't even know she'd helped me. So how would Marinda? It's not like the old lady knew anything about her or Dr Rears. Unless Marinda thought Mrs Timpson had called the police earlier that day. Maybe she had seen us watching through the window.

I was sitting outside my mum's house. The key was in the ignition, but the car was off. I was on my way to see Aaron before picking up Joshua. He was still at his dad's and was so excited to be coming home.

I needed to check on Aaron first. I wasn't sure I would be allowed near him, but I needed to try. I willed myself to move and finally turned the key. My legs were like jelly, but I compelled them to spring into action anyway. *Left foot down, push the car into gear, right foot down.* I talked to myself in the same manner all the way to the hospital. *Just get there. He will be okay.*

I spent ten minutes trying to find a place to park. Parking made me nervous at the best of times, but the hospital car park was always so busy. I finally found someone pulling out and I took their space and rushed to the reception of the A&E department to explain who I was looking for. The lady behind the desk was kind and plump. She led me to a small, empty waiting room and explained someone would be with me shortly. *You're here now. He will be okay.* After a few long minutes, a doctor appeared. She introduced herself as Dr Jasani.

"Are you related to Aaron?" she asked.

"I'm his girlfriend, we live together," I lied. I'd lied so much it was coming easily to me.

"Oh. Well, he was in pretty terrible shape when he arrived. He was stabbed in the abdomen, but we have stemmed the bleeding. He was lucky, and the knife didn't hit any organs. We've sutured the wound, and he is stable for now."

"Oh, thank God." The tears flowed. I hadn't realised how close they were.

"He isn't awake yet, but do you want to see him?"

"Yes! Yes, please."

She took me on a short walk down the corridor and into a private room on the left. Aaron was lying on the bed with his eyes closed. The machine next to him beeped steadily. His phone and wallet were next to him on the bedside table.

The doctor left me to sit with him and told me to call the nurses if he woke up. There was a stack of two small plastic chairs in the room's corner. I took the top one and placed it next to Aaron. His chest rose and fell rhythmically, and the machines beeping periodically. I placed my hand on his, unsure what to do or say. Scenes of people on TV talking to people in comas swam through my mind.

"I'm sorry, Aaron." It came out as a whisper. "I'm so sorry. You're safe now."

I watched him for a quarter of an hour. His eyes twitched now and then, but they didn't open. I didn't want to leave him, but I needed to get Joshua.

"I'll be back tomorrow," I told him and kissed his cheek.

His skin was warmer than I thought it would be. As I reached the door, I heard a ringing noise. His machine? I spun around and walked back to him. The sound was coming from his phone. I grabbed it, hoping it was a relative calling, and suddenly remembered my promise to call his mum. The number flashed up, so it wasn't a number he had saved in his phone. Disappointment hit me, but I answered anyway, in case it was important.

"Hello?" I sounded businesslike and in no mood for sales calls.

"Hello, this is DI Swanson. I'm looking for Aaron Walker."

"DI Swanson? It's Summer."

"Summer? Why are you answering this phone?"

"It's Aarons'. He's in hospital. He's the friend Marinda stabbed, remember? Why are you ringing him? He's not able to talk yet."

He was silent for a moment. "Well, I shouldn't say. I'll explain when we see you."

"No, please, I can't take anymore waiting. We aren't meeting until tomorrow. I can't wait until then. Please." My voice verged on hysterical.

He sighed loudly. "Look, we're trying to find Mrs Timpson's relatives. This number was written on a piece of paper next to her house phone. I thought it was her son's number. There are pictures of her with him all around the house."

The realisation hit me hard. *My* m*um...Mum.* I heard Aaron's voice in my mind as he called out to me, lying bleeding in my doorway. He'd known exactly where Marinda was going. Mrs Timpson was his mum.

49

Summer

Two days later, I was in the hospital with Aaron. He sat propped up in his bed, still in the private ward. I sat next to him again in the plastic chair. Some colour had returned to his cheeks, and his hair fell in a mess around his face. He was doing better now that the police had caught Marinda. Though, he was devastated about his mum, as was I. He could finally talk about what happened. A couple of weeks ago, he had spotted *Emma* taking Lucy out even though she had no approved leave. He'd asked Emma about it. He had always liked Emma and got on well with her, so he was shocked when she got nasty with him and told him to mind his own business. She initially threatened to tell the police he'd raped her.

"But you didn't!" I stupidly said. He smiled sadly at me.

"Of course not, but I was scared. Even with no proof, an accusation like that can destroy a man's life. I would have been sacked, regardless."

"Christ," I muttered because there was nothing else to say. He was right.

"The same day you asked me about Lucy, Emma had come to speak to me." His eyes were glazed over, as if he wanted to get the words out but didn't want to feel the emotions attached to them. "She showed me a picture on her phone. It was my mum in the garden. She said nothing, but smiled at me. I asked her what the fuck she thought she was doing. She said 'Lucy never existed no matter who asks' and then she walked away."

"I'm so sorry I didn't try to call your mum after you were stabbed. I was so worried about getting to my own mum that I didn't even think."

"It's not your fault, Summer." He squeezed my hand. He sniffed, and a lone tear fell from his cheek. "Emma, or Marinda, whatever the bitch's name is, would have gone missing and turned up later to do it. They caught her thanks to you." He paused before adding, "I'm so sorry I lied to you. I didn't know what to say or what to do. I knew if you asked too many questions, she would threaten you too. At first, I thought she'd hurt Lucy. Killed her or something."

"How did you know where Lucy was staying?" I asked.

"Lucy found me. She followed me home one day and turned up at my door. I nearly had a stroke." A stilted laugh escaped him. "When you said you had seen her, I assumed it was because she wanted to know where you lived. I didn't know if it was to hurt you or what." He tried to shrug his shoulders but winced at the pain.

"Did she try to hurt you?"

"No. She said she needed help." He looked away guiltily. "I told her to fuck off at first. I was so worried about my mum. But a bit later she put a note through my door with a mobile number on it. I rang her eventually. I told her I'd help her. She didn't trust me then, though. She said she would only trust you."

I nodded. I knew he was finally telling me the truth. I wasn't even annoyed anymore that he'd lied. I understood. Lucy was back in the hospital now, although I hadn't seen her. I'd told my mum the whole story. Dr Rears had been arrested again and was no doubt loudly protesting his innocence. He had admitted Marinda ordered him to get close to my mum, though she never said why. I assumed it was to threaten me. He'd worked with Marinda because of her threats to tell everyone about his affair with Aaliyah. I didn't actually see him do anything to Louise, and with so little evidence, he could easily walk free. Thankfully, he wouldn't practice again. Like Aaron had said, the accusation alone would ruin him. At least we could get Marinda on an attempted murder *and* a murder charge for stabbing Aaron and his mum. She should be put away for a long time. I hadn't yet told Mum what she had said about Eddie not actually being ill, but I planned to soon.

"How are you feeling?" I asked him, feeling silly but unsure of what else to say.

He grinned at me with his uneven teeth. "Been better physically! But now I'm free of that psycho bitch. At least I know no one else will get hurt. I wish I'd said something sooner or got Mum away somewhere safe."

"I should have realised what was happening sooner," I said, on the verge of tears. I looked down to hide my welling eyes. "I'm handing my notice in. I'm no advocate."

"Summer, look at me." Aaron leaned over and raised my head with his hand. "You did exactly what you were supposed to. More even than most people would have done in your position. You were Lucy's confidante, her voice. You were there for her when no one else was and when she was at her lowest. Ill, terrified, and alone. Even after she bopped you over the head and knocked you clean out! You are an amazing advocate."

***

Later that day, Joshua laid on the sofa with his head in my lap. I stroked his head gently, never wanting to move. Toy Story played on the TV as we cuddled, and I finally felt safe. Until a knock at the door made us both jump. Anyone wanting to visit needed to press the buzzer on the outside door before gaining access to the building, so who the hell was knocking on my door? I stayed still. Joshua turned and looked up at me.

"Who's banging on the door, Mummy?" His bottom lip pouted in annoyance at the interruption.

"Not sure, baby." I smiled despite the terror which gripped me like a vice. "I'll go check."

He sat up and moved over to lie down on the other side of the sofa. I rose and walked out as if everything was normal, and stood in the hallway to survey the door. The possibilities ran through my mind. Lucy was in the hospital. Marinda was in custody. Aaron was in the hospital. Mum never visited. Kelly would have called. There was no way I was opening it. I could look through the peephole, but to be frank, I didn't want to. I tugged my phone out to see if I had any missed calls from Kelly. There was nothing, other than a notification about the weather. *Knock. Knock. Knock.*

"Mummy, get the door!" Joshua whined from the living

room.

"I'm on my way," I lied as I stared at my phone, wondering who to call.

A buzzing noise from the phone almost made me drop it to the ground. I checked the number, unknown.

The familiar anxiety came creeping back into the pit of my stomach. I was unsure whether to answer, until I realised I recognised the number after all. I quickly accepted the call before they hung up.

"Hello?" I said warily in case I was wrong.

"Hi, Ms Thomas. DI Swanson here."

Relief washed over me. I'd been right. "Hi," I said as I gathered myself. I put my hand to my chest, trying to calm my pounding heart.

"Er, I've just knocked on your door. Are you in? Someone let me through the main door when I arrived. I realised after knocking twice that I should have called first…" He trailed off.

I didn't answer him. Instead, I walked forward and finally swung open the door. There he was. The top of my head barely grazed his chest now that I was bare-footed. I was so relieved I actually laughed, much to his perplexion.

"Hi," I repeated. "You scared me half to death."

"Er…Hi. I'm sorry. May I come in for a moment?"

"Sure." I stood aside to let him in and closed the door behind him. I led him through into the kitchen. "Would you like a drink?" I offered, cursing myself for not picking up milk. He'd probably want tea like everyone else in this country.

"Water, please. I don't drink hot drinks."

"Oh! Really?"

"Yes." He looked sheepish. "Bit awkward when everyone you question offers you tea."

"Yes, I know the feeling. I don't drink hot drinks either." My heart said this was another reason we were well suited. My brain told it to shut up.

"Oh." He looked surprised.

"I don't like them, other than hot chocolate with cream and marshmallows." I made a mental note to get some milk so I could make me and Joshua hot chocolate later. We could drink it before bed, whilst watching yet another film or playing a board game. As if he read my thoughts, Joshua came flying into the kitchen right at that moment. He stopped dead in the doorway and positioned his big blue eyes directly on the intimidating Swanson, who suddenly looked like a rabbit caught in headlights. I suppressed a giggle.

"Hi, little fella," he eventually said.

"I'm not little. I'm big." Joshua huffed, eyebrows knitted, bottom lip out.

"Joshua, this is Detective Swanson," I told him, emphasizing the word detective. His grumpy face lit up, and he was all smiles suddenly.

"Detective? Do you catch bad people? Like…bank robbers? Or people who take toys? Or cars? I heard sometimes people take cars. Mummy said so, and she said people also take things from cars, so I must not leave things out on the seat. And what about chickens?"

"Chickens?" Swanson gave me a baffled look. I laughed out loud, as did Joshua.

"Joshua, give me a hug." I diffused the situation before he chased Swanson away. He came running to me and squeezed me tight. I kissed his soft hair. "Now go watch the film while I talk to the detective. I'll bring you a snack, okay?"

"Okay, Mummy." He ran off again to the lounge.

SUMMER

"Chickens?" Swanson asked again. I shrugged my shoulders as I poured a glass of water. I had no idea what the kid was talking about.

"Who knows?" I passed him the glass of water. "What brings you round?"

"Well, it's a little awkward, which is why I came in person." He paused and looked at me, looked *down* at me, I should say.

"Go on…"

"If you don't want to know, that's fine, you can say. It's no skin off my nose, but I thought I'd offer." He raised his hands as if in surrender.

"Go on…" I repeated, wishing he'd spit it out.

"I know where your brother is," he finally said.

"Oh."

"But like I said, only if you want to know?"

"Well, yes, of course. Thank you. How come you know where he is?"

"We need to know if he has seen Marinda. She's blaming him. Saying that he told her the devil was after her and she needed to kill his family."

"Oh."

"You're saying that a lot." He smiled at me, and I smiled back. I didn't know what else to say. "Well, maybe think about it and let me know if you want the address."

"Is he in a hospital, still? Or is he out?"

"He's in a hospital."

"Oh."

Swanson laughed. "You need to expand your vocabulary."

I laughed too because I didn't know what else to say. Did I want to see my brother? Someone had to deal with the mess Marinda had created. He needed to know what she'd told me about his hallucinations. If he didn't know already. But did I want to open up more wounds and get deeper into this mess? Part of me wanted to be selfish for once and let the police deal with it.

"I'll think about it," I said.

"Sure, call me when you're ready."

"Has Marinda said anything else about why she wanted to hurt us?"

"No, she seems to be playing ill."

"Well, I would say she thought it all through pretty well!" I scoffed. Marinda was not ill. She knew right from wrong.

"I agree. We can catch up about it soon, but I'd better go, lots to do."

"Sure." I smiled, though I wished he'd stay.

I walked him to the door, and we said our goodbyes. He would be in touch soon regarding the case, anyway. Then I grabbed a packet of biscuits and went back to sit with Joshua again. He curled his skinny body right into mine as we lay on the sofa watching the film, eating biscuits, and thinking about getting milk for hot chocolate. A normal family again, doing normal things. That was what I needed from life, what Joshua needed. My brother stayed on my mind, and I knew I had to help him. He needed me, too. Not today, though. I curled around Joshua even tighter. At that moment, the two of us were enough. Tomorrow, though, who knew?

About the Author

Ashley is a thirty-something mother of one living in Nottingham in the UK. She is half Irish and half English and brought up between the two countries - so has the pleasure of knowing both well. She grew up in a family of eight and has been writing ever since she can remember. She had a little typewriter by the age of six and wrote full stories most weekends, as well as devouring hundreds of books.

She went on to study psychology, gaining both a first class degree and a masters in Health Psychology. She has won awards for her work in mental health and was once nominated for Volunteer of the Year for her voluntary work with the Brain Injury Association. She has also worked as a Mental Health Support Worker, a Care Assistant within stroke and an Independent Advocate. All of her work experience heavily features in her creepy psychological thriller novels, She see's stories in everyday life just waiting to be told and writes in a thrilling way that keeps the reader guessing until the end. In December 2020, she created the blog Crazy About Writing to help other authors showcase their writing skills. She also uses her platform to promote writing within the local community through competitions for kids and blogging opportunities for teenagers.

She loves interacting with fans on Twitter, Facebook, Insta

or TikTok so give her a follow and get involved! Don't forget to subscribe to the newsletter and receive regular updates, exclusive content and be the first to know about new books!

You can connect with me on:
- https://www.ashleybeeganauthor.com
- https://twitter.com/AshleyBeegan
- https://www.facebook.com/AshleyBeegan
- https://www.instagram.com/ashleybeegan

Subscribe to my newsletter:
- https://www.ashleybeeganauthor.com

Also by Ashley Beegan

Order book two of the Detective Swanson series now!

Mother...Liar...Murderer
Someone believes Astrid has a **dark** secret. One which would completely destroy her perfect life.

And they will do anything to get her to admit to it.

But fiery Astrid doesn't take kindly to threats, and when she finally realises who is terrorising her, she makes a decision she will never recover from.

A decision which has far worse consequences than any secrets from her past.

Printed in Great Britain
by Amazon